THE VISCOUNT'S DARING CINDERELLA
DAMSEL IN DISTRESS
BOOK IV

HAYLEIGH MILLS

DARKAN PRESS

The Viscount's Daring Cinderella is a work of fiction. While reference might be made to actual historical events or existing locations, the names, characters, places, and incidents are either the product of the author's imagination or are used fictitiously, and any resemblance to actual persons, living or dead, business establishments, events, or locales are entirely coincidental.

All rights reserved. No part of this book may be reproduced in any form by any electronic or mechanical means—except in the case of brief quotations embodied in critical articles or reviews —without written permission.

For information regarding subsidiary rights, please contact the Publisher: Darkanpress@gmail.com

First Edition March 2024

Edited by AuthorsDesigns
Proofread by Jeanne Olynick
Cover Art by Forever After Romance Designs
Cover design and Formatting by AuthorsDesigns

Copyright © 2024 by Hayleigh Mills

CHAPTER 1

Chalfont House, Buckinghamshire

Lady Beryl Keene stooped by the lake and dipped her hand into its cool depths. She needed this. The space, quiet, and relaxation. She was not one for embroidery or needlework. It was early in the morning, but she could already feel the warm promise of the day. Beryl splashed her hands across the surface and watched as the ripples came ashore. A light breeze hit the water, and the ripples died as soon as they came. If only she, too, could disappear and never have to face her worries.

Beryl sighed. The water felt cool and refreshing. She could never tire of it. The lake was her escape from Chalfont House, her spoilt cousins, and their ever-demanding mother. Lady Ellsworth was widowed, but fortunately for her cousins, they had a brother who inherited the estate, so they would never have to suffer the indignities she had to endure.

The lake was where Beryl could find calm and bring peace to her otherwise miserable existence. She could cool down whenever she was upset and think of more positive things. She frequently fantasized that she was safe and content in her childhood home. Her days were often so dismal that all Beryl had were her dreams, and she could not bear to part with them. If she gave up on her dreams, what would she have left?

The water looked so inviting, and she wanted to wade in it, but surely, she should not. Beryl stood up. *Why the heck not?* She smiled and slowly put her hand behind her to loosen her dress. She had become adept at undressing herself since she moved to Chalfont House.

A thick copse of trees shielded the lake on both sides, which offered a great deal of privacy, and she had never encountered anyone on her rides there before. There was a fallen log close by, and Beryl neatly folded and placed her clothes on top of the log. The last thing she wanted was for her clothes to get wet. Garbed in only her shift, she quickly walked into the lake.

"Wonderful," she murmured.

She relished the feeling as the cool water lapped at her feet. When she was waist-deep, Beryl started swimming across the lake. *Refreshing.* She did not need to worry about her cousins missing her, for they were rarely up before ten in the morning. They were not particularly concerned about how she spent her time before they had breakfast, but afterward, they demanded her attention.

Beryl's hair was in a braid, and she would pin it up once she returned to the house. She certainly did not want her cousins to discover she had stripped and gone for a swim. Beryl dived beneath the water and emerged, feeling invigorated. She lay on her back, stretched out her arms and legs and tilted her chin. She took a deep breath and relaxed until she felt weightless. She promised herself not to let anything toss her into disorder today.

Beryl turned over and dipped below the surface once more. She swam around in circles and alternated between floating and swimming. After a few minutes, Beryl felt a sense of unease and a prickling on the back of her neck. Her heart lurched. She sensed she was not alone. Small bumps raised along her arms, and a cold shiver ran down her spine. Beryl built up the courage to turn around to see who was there. She slowly scanned the trees. She found the culprit. He was sitting atop a majestic beast, and his gaze was piercing. Beryl was conscious of the shift clinging to all her curves, and she quickly sank into the water until only her head was visible.

"Have you lost all sense of propriety, good sir?" Beryl demanded.

A heavy silence fell. She discerned that he was a gentleman because of his well-tailored clothing made of luxurious fabric and his horse. Her heart pounded in her chest, and she prayed that her voice did not shake.

"What have I done to cause you to accuse me of being improper?" he drawled with an air of confidence.

Beryl cocked her head and raised a brow. "You dare to ask?"

The rogue chuckled. "I do. It seems to me that you are the one to invite scrutiny. After all, you are bathing almost naked in plain view."

Beryl gasped, outrage and mortification burning through her. Although he did not say it, his tone implied that she had asked a ridiculous question considering her precarious position. She narrowed her gaze at him, carefully thinking about a scathing retort, and it was then that Beryl realized how handsome he was. She could tell that he was tall, even seated on his mount. He had a broad chest and shoulders, a narrow waist, black hair, and a straight nose.

He was too far away to see the color of his eyes but not far enough to escape them boring into her. Interestingly, the shade of his complexion was a bit darker than she would expect, and she concluded he must have returned from a country with a warmer climate. He was certainly a scoundrel to stare at her so, but he stole her breath. A most peculiar sensation fluttered low in her belly. Beryl realized she had been staring, and her face grew hot before her entire body followed suit. She was sure her body heat warmed the water around her.

Although the rogue was right, she was almost naked; Beryl was stunned that he would say such a thing. A gentleman should have kept such thoughts to himself. His beauty was matched only by his brazenness. Beryl felt another flutter in her stomach, and her cheeks burned brighter.

"Have I stolen your ability to speak?"

The rogue! Beryl frowned. "I find your actions to

be highly improper, sir. Should you not have left as soon as you assessed the situation? I cannot think of an acceptable reason for you to be spying—"

His lips twisted into a cynical smile. "*Spying?*"

His voice filled with incredulity.

Beryl sniffed. "You *were* secretly observing me during a private moment. Were you not?" Beryl asked with a significant lifting of her brow.

His expression held a hint of mockery. "My lady, you do not grasp the meaning of the word private. If you would swim in the lake with your wet shift clinging to every curve, I do not believe it is privacy you want."

Beryl inhaled sharply. He spoke as if he was stating something quite obvious. Handsome, arrogant, and wicked. When she breathed out, it was somewhat strangled. She was livid.

How dare he!

She was mortified that he would speak to her in this way. A moment's silence hung heavy between them. Beryl gave him a hard, cold gaze. "Are you implying that I want *your* attention?"

Beryl was sure to make her voice drip with scorn. He was insufferably rude. She most certainly did not desire his scrutiny and forwardness. She could not bear the thought of being discovered in such a situation and could not even begin to think how she would explain it. Her governess had taught her well. One of the golden rules was to avoid gentlemen to whom she had not been introduced. Furthermore, she should not be alone with a gentleman and certainly not one who looks as predatory as this handsome devil.

The rake shrugged his powerful shoulders and smirked.

Beryl gave him a withering stare. "If that is what you believe, let me disabuse you of the notion, sir. You are sorely mistaken. The way that I see it …" Beryl paused. Her hands were trembling but thank goodness he could not see it. "If you had a shred of decency, you would turn your horse around and go about your business. I did not seek you out."

The corners of his lips raised in a sardonic smile. "You wish for me to leave?"

Beryl's heart fluttered at his smile. She looked away swiftly. What the devil was wrong with her? "I do," she answered firmly. The fluttering did not dissipate.

His expression stilled and grew serious. Beryl was stunned for the second time when the rogue replied, "Your wish is my command, my lady."

He wheeled his horse around and, without a backward glance, rode onto a path among the trees. Beryl did not leave the water immediately, although she desperately wanted to. She thought it best to wait to be sure he had, in fact, departed. Sitting there for so long was probably foolish, but she could not be sure he was not lurking in the woods. Watching and waiting.

She also had to get back to the house and make herself presentable. Beryl did not wish to invite any mockery or snide remarks from her cousins. She had suffered enough from that. A few more minutes passed, and all seemed quiet. She quickly waded from the lake, took her clothes, and hid behind a stout tree while she dressed. The rogue did not reappear, and she breathed a sigh of relief. She mounted her horse post-haste and rode toward Chalfont House. Beryl reflected on his words. She should be concerned about any possible blemish to her character, yet she found she was intrigued.

Who was this man?

How could such a rake have a sensual appeal? She had not forgotten how hot she had flushed under his intense gaze and the sensation as it flowed through her body. Taking a steady breath, she pushed away all thoughts of that stranger. Beryl felt a pang of loneliness at the thought of returning to the house. An oppressive feeling always surrounded her once she entered, especially when faced with her cousins' spitefulness and indifference to her circumstances. In truth, they took some pleasure in reminding her she depended on their generosity to live.

She had always dreamed of having a season, courting, getting married and having children. To say that Beryl had fallen on hard times would be an understatement. She doubted that there would be any prospects of her dream becoming a reality. It had been eight months since her father passed away and she was officially out of mourning, but what dressing in black had to do with the pain that stabbed at her heart? She was in mourning still and missed her father terribly.

Beryl sighed heavily. She vividly remembered when her father became ill. She had been full of hope, believing he would soon recover. She did not know it then, but it had been the beginning of the end of her dreams. Her father was the only close relative Beryl had, which made his passing even more painful. She had never felt more isolated and alone. When he was alive, he loved and cherished her. He did not need to say the words. She had always felt his love.

When he first became ill, Beryl could not bear to be parted from him and had entertained no such conversation. He had wanted her to have a season, but she would hardly enjoy it when he was lying in bed. He had insisted that she leave him, but she steadfastly refused. Beryl recalled how determined she was to wait until he recovered before going to town. She had seen the defeat in his eyes, and finally he gave up on asking her to go.

In hindsight she wondered if he had known he was no longer for this world. She was happy she remained with him until the end. At first, her father's joints were swollen, and he was in terrible pain. The physician said it was gout and that he would soon recover. Unfortunately, he did not. He had passed away in his sleep one night. Beryl's eyes shimmered with tears as she remembered finding him pale and lifeless that morning. She recalled thinking it was not possible. *How could it be? How could he be gone?* When she confronted the physician, he simply said her father's heart gave out.

Her world had imploded.

The estate was bequeathed to Mr. Jasper Haskell, a distant cousin, who insisted she leave the estate immediately for reasons she did not understand. Mr. Haskell did not have the courtesy to face her and deliver the news in person. Rather, he sent her a letter. When she opened it, Beryl quickly realized how her circumstances had changed.

She was without power and any connections of her own.

Yet, she did not immediately accept that her father had not provided for her. They had never discussed it, and she just assumed that he would have. He was, after all, a responsible man. If the letter was to be believed, her father had not made any provisions for her before he died, and he had not taken any actions to protect her. *Incredulous.* Beryl had sent a letter by return to her cousin demanding he provide an explanation. At the very least she should have an inheritance from her mother's dowry.

The response had been swift and crushing. There was nothing for her bar a few pieces of jewelry that belonged to her mother. Beryl's fall from grace was complete. She reasoned that it must have been because her father thought he would have more time to put his affairs in order. It was the only thing that made any sense. She did not want to be angry with her father. She was one and twenty, veritably on the shelf by society's standards, and those less charitable would refer to her as an old maid. Beryl had been filled with anxiety when she considered her future. She did not know what the devil she was going to do for Mr. Haskell made it clear that he was not the least bit concerned with her circumstances.

While her trunks were being packed for her departure to some unknown destination, she had received a letter from another cousin, Lady Edith Ellsworth. Beryl had almost collapsed in relief, but little did she know Lady Ellsworth was not her savior.

She is my tormentor.

Taking a steady breath, Beryl drew on the reins of her mount, dismounted, and handed him over to the stable lad. She stood in the forecourt for a few beats, staring at the large oak door.

The memory of her first time in this house was as vivid as if it happened yesterday. When Beryl had arrived at Chalfont House, she was ushered into the drawing room where Lady Ellsworth had received her. The room was as dark as the scowl on her cousin's face.

Lady Ellsworth had snorted, then said, "I never

took your father for a wastrel but there you have it. Here you are before me, the daughter of a marquess with no dowry, and no prospect of finding a husband."

Lady Ellsworth's chuckle had contained no mirth. Goosebumps pricked Beryl's arms, and she had felt cold despite the fire roaring in the fireplace.

"Your mother thought she was better than us. She never came here when I invited her. If only she could see you now. How the mighty have fallen."

Lady Ellsworth's voice had not masked her pleasure. It was as though she had waited a long time to utter those words in triumph. By this twisted logic, her mother was humbled even in death.

"If I had not sent for you, where would you be?" Lady Ellsworth asked, with furrowed brows and stern lips.

"I am grateful that you sent for me, Lady Ellsworth, for I do not know the answer to your question," Beryl had replied as she dropped her eyes.

An unpleasant, self-conscious emotion had gripped her, and she felt terribly exposed and powerless. *Shame*. That was what she'd felt.

"Fortunately, for you, I decided to take on this

burden. I am a charitable woman with a good heart. You will not give me cause to regret it."

People who are kind and charitable did not need to say so. It was demonstrated by their deeds. Beryl had begun to get a sense of things to come at Chalfont House, and she had felt dread for she had no other choice.

"Certainly not, Lady Ellsworth. I will be above reproach."

"Your belongings are being unpacked, and shortly you will be able to retire to your room."

Lady Ellsworth sniffed as her eyes had traveled from Beryl's head to her feet. "You will not live a life of luxury here. You have been saved from goodness knows what, so I expect you to show me your gratitude. Your cousins, Grace and Estelle have gone for a visit, and you will meet them when they return. Your cousin Lord Ellsworth is at Oxford."

"I look forward to meeting them," Beryl had said, beginning the stage of her polite façade in the face of such spite.

"You are here to be a companion for Grace and Estelle. You will assist with whatever it is that they need, including preparing their clothing and dressing them, if necessary. They have maids, but

THE VISCOUNT'S DARING CINDERELLA

they may prefer you do it, and you will oblige. You will not have a maid, so I am sure you will be quite adept at dressing them in no time. You will be guided by your cousins regarding whatever activities they would like to pursue."

Beryl's breath had caught in her throat. She had never been without a maid and certainly never dressed herself, but she would learn. "I would be happy to assist in whatever way I can, Lady Ellsworth."

Her voice had not betrayed the dejection she felt, but her heart slumped.

Lady Ellsworth's smile had been tight and her eyes narrowed in censure. "I was not asking you if you were happy. I was merely stating what you are expected to do so we do not have *any* misunderstanding."

"As you wish, Lady Ellsworth."

There had been a knock on the door.

"Come in," Lady Ellsworth said.

A maid entered and curtsied. "The room is prepared, Lady Ellsworth."

"Thank you, Daisy."

"I will show you to your room."

Lady Ellsworth stood and walked from the room. Beryl had followed closely behind, observing the house was tastefully furnished but it lacked warmth. They ascended the stairs and walked down the hallway until they approached a room where the door stood open. Lady Ellsworth stepped inside and Beryl followed. Her trunks had been unpacked and her jewelry box sat atop the dressing table.

Lady Ellsworth's eyes squinted and narrowed in on the box. "What do we have here?"

Lady Ellsworth opened the jewelry box and spread each piece on the dressing table.

"These are quite lovely pieces," Lady Ellsworth remarked as she chose a ruby necklace and studied it with care.

Her chest tight, Beryl had said, "Thank you. They are all that I have remaining from my mother, and they hold great sentimental value."

Lady Ellsworth spun around with such speed that Beryl had lurched back.

"Sentimental value?"

"Yes. I do not have anything else—"

"And what are you contributing to your stay here at Chalfont House?" Lady Ellsworth cut her off. "Sacrificing a necklace is the least that you can do. You ungrateful girl."

Beryl had been stunned into silence, and the familiar feeling of shame returned, but this time it was tinged with sadness. Lady Ellsworth's short and stubby fingers were wrapped tightly around the necklace. Beryl had to give it up. This was the only place she had to lay her head until she could make sense of her life.

"As you wish, Lady Ellsworth."

"You will do to remember how fortunate you are to have a roof over your head," Lady Ellsworth said as she left the room and closed the door behind her. Beryl had walked up to the dressing table and placed the rest of her jewelry back in its place. Tears streamed down her face and splashed into the box.

That day had been the beginning of her misery at Chalfont House.

Pushing aside those awful memories and squaring her shoulders, Beryl braced herself for another day of cruel taunts that unfortunately had the power to strike her heart. She knew living like this could not be sustained.

Oh, but I must endure until I've formed a plan.

CHAPTER 2

Lord Theodore Godwin, Viscount Bowden, had a smile fixed on his lips as he rode toward Bowden Park. He wondered who the chit was. The young lady who had carelessly discarded her dress to wade unabashed in the lake. Well, unabashed until she discovered he was watching. If looks had the power to kill, he would most certainly be dead. He chuckled. She was fiery, that one. The thought of the shift clinging to her wet body stirred his blood.

Theodore spurred his horse forward. He had just returned from another jaunt in Italy, and the weather had been fantastic. Now that he was back at Bowden House, he picked up his old habit of an early morning ride. He had not expected to see anyone, much less a lady, at this early hour. Usually, he would not encounter anyone except the odd villager here and there.

When he sat by the lake, he always felt blessed to behold its beauty. He was hopeful for his future yet rebellious against what was expected of him. The lake was his peaceful place, and he had not thought to share it with anyone. He was more keenly aware of nature when he was there. The aromas of nature were somehow intoxicating when its depths surrounded him. He could hear the birds chirping happily, and when he took the air in his nostrils, it always seemed so fresh.

The cool breeze caressed Theodore's cheeks as he spurred his horse from a canter to a gallop. Even the quick dash was not enough to make him forget the young lady. How could he forget her? If he were asked to describe her in one word, it would be stunning.

She was exceptionally beautiful with blonde hair, a pert nose, full lips, and doe eyes that could not mask her innocence. Somehow, he sensed she was not prideful about her beauty, yet she exuded an air of confidence. When she turned over to float, he saw the outline of her firm breasts as the fabric was molded to her body. His cock had stirred, and he wondered what it would feel like if he could only just …

Theodore's thoughts were disrupted because that was when she caught him. Truth be told, he was a bit embarrassed to be caught gawking like an untried lad. He should have remained behind the tree line, but he had felt mesmerized by her daring. He wanted to get a closer look.

It was not just her beauty. Beautiful ladies were a dime a dozen. She stimulated his curiosity with her boldness in swimming in the lake and challenging him without hesitation. Most of the ladies he met were nothing but polite and agreed with everything he said. It could be dreadfully boring. Others were downright disagreeable for no reason he could discern, but not this chit. She seemed a bit more interesting. He wondered what she would have done if he had refused to leave or, better yet, if he had stolen her clothes. Theodore grinned wickedly as he rode out from among the trees into the clearing.

Theodore was approaching Bowden Park, and as he rode closer, he could see that a carriage awaited him. When he moved closer, he was finally able to recognize the insignia.

Damn it to hell! What was his uncle, Lord Amos Merton, doing here?

His uncle could hardly know that he was back from his sojourn. It was impossible for the news to travel that fast. Theodore would not have to wait long to find out what he wanted. He dismounted, handed over his horse to the stable lad and walked to the main entrance. Theodore entered the house where his valet was waiting with a basin and towel for him to wash his hands. Afterward, he went directly to the drawing room, pushing the door open to find his uncle having a cup of tea. Merton had certainly made himself comfortable.

"Merton, it is kind of you to visit," Theodore said politely.

It was anything but. Theodore had to keep up the farce because he did not want to alienate his uncle. He had spoken with more kindness than he felt. It was not that he disliked his uncle. He just found him irritating and interfering.

"Bowden, there you are. I was beginning to wonder if you had gone on another jaunt to Europe," Merton quipped as he pinned Theodore with his gaze.

One would think his uncle had a dry sense of

humor, but Theodore knew better. His uncle did not have a humorous bone in his body, dry or otherwise. Merton hid his barbs as he tried to be subtle and clever. He had failed. Miserably. Theodore would ignore the barb as he always did. He was usually happy and cheerful. Cheerfully irresponsible, some may say.

Theodore gazed at his uncle. "What brings you to Bowden?" He had to ask since Merton volunteered no information.

"I thought that since you abandoned your nieces, I should at least check upon them. After all, I am *concerned* about their wellbeing," Merton responded matter-of-factly.

Here we go again, Theodore thought with frustration. How dare he imply Theodore was not concerned about his nieces' welfare. Worse, he sensed the proverbial lecture about responsibility coming. Theodore had heard it all before, and he was sure by now Merton knew that he was wasting his time. Theodore did not know why his uncle bothered at all. Perhaps he was mad because he gave Theodore the same lecture each time they met, although there was no change in Theodore's attitude.

"I hardly abandoned them, Merton," Theodore

said politely. "All their needs are met, and they are well cared for here at Bowden Park."

"So, you believe if they are housed and fed, *that* is the extent of your duty. You are then free to traipse around Europe and live a life of debauchery. You should be ashamed of yourself," Merton said with a hint of moral superiority.

"I am not doing anything out of the ordinary. I am doing exactly what any other young gentleman of my age is doing. Nothing more, nothing less," Theodore replied firmly as he tried to hide his irritation.

Theodore would rather not have this conversation, not now or ever. He realized that he was famished as he had not had any sustenance before going for the ride. He poured himself a cup of tea and selected one of the pastries. He took a bite, chewed, and savored the taste before his uncle spoke again and ruined his appetite.

Merton huffed. "Your brother must be turning in his grave. Those children have lost both their father and their mother. Did you not promise your bother that you would care for them as if they were your own? Is this how you do it?" Merton demanded.

The mention of his brother, William, and the promise he made was like a punch in the gut. William was older than Theodore's five and twenty, and he was the favored son. It was not just that he had been the firstborn; William was everything Theodore was not. William was responsible, caring, and considerate. When they were young, they constantly competed, or should Theodore say that he competed with William. William had been the best at everything he tried and always came out on top. He married young and had a beautiful wife and two daughters.

Although Theodore had been a little jealous of William, he loved his brother unquestioningly. Somehow, William understood him. The good and the bad. William never judged him for any of his conduct. Theodore knew that he wanted to be a free agent from a very young age. He wanted to liberate himself from societal strictures and act outside them, and he had done just that. Being free to do as he pleased was entrenched in him, and he did not fight it but rather embraced all the pleasure.

William had made him promise that if anything should ever happen, Theodore was to take care of his nieces. He had felt compelled to agree because he was the closest relative and the most likely option. There were no other siblings. He did not particularly like children, but he remembered the look on William's face when he had asked him. Back then, Theodore could not imagine his brother, who was so full of life, would be taken from him. Now, his nieces were in his charge, and he felt quite ill-prepared for the undertaking. Theodore had always thought that William's burden was a lot to bear, although he, too, was the son of a nobleman.

Theodore could feel his temper rising. He was not totally without honor. "Did you come here to scold me, Merton?" he demanded.

His uncle sighed heavily. "I came here to check on the children. I was not expecting to see you. So, scold you, no. Remind you of your duty, absolutely."

"The estate is well managed, and there is nothing that concerns me," Theodore replied tersely.

Merton gave him a level gaze and persisted, "Your place is *here*, Bowden. I am not opposed to a young gentleman having some distraction, but decadent parties cannot be your focus. You should be thinking about taking a wife."

Did Merton say that he was not opposed? Theodore thought he must have misheard. He was way beyond needing his uncle's approval or validation.

Theodore sighed heavily, scrubbing a hand over his face. "I do not wish to wed."

Merton's gaze bored into him, and he waved a hand in dismissal. "What nonsense! It would be best if you had an heir. Who will inherit the estate if you do not wed, and you were to unfortunately die."

His uncle had legitimate concerns, but this would not sway Theodore. His nieces would not inherit, and he supposed the law was such because if ladies inherited an estate, the family name associated with the land and house would die, being replaced by her husband's. The aristocrats could not countenance losing it all because their daughter married a stranger.

Regardless, Theodore was not inclined to change his mind. He had been the spare to a viscountcy all his life, and he hated the restrictions imposed on his elder brother as he was groomed to be the heir. Tragically, William's life ended too soon, and though his brother seemed happy with his domesticity, he never got to truly live.

Being the heir had never appealed to Theodore, and he did not want the burden that came with a title. Now that he had it, he would damn well still live as how he pleased. Theodore needed to say something to appease his uncle and end this undesirable conversation. "You will be pleased to know I will attend the social events this season," Theodore said.

The corner of his uncle's lips lifted into a smile. "Bloody marvelous!"

Theodore gazed into Merton's eyes. "I will not commit further."

"Who knows? You may meet a young lady worthy of your attention," Merton said with a smile, nodding his approval.

Theodore's mind was instantly filled with images of the young lady he met earlier. He was certain she was a lady because of how she spoke and her self-possession. She was certainly worthy of his attention. Just not in the way that his uncle imagined. Theodore wondered if she frequented the lake. It was likely because she looked comfortable there and did not seem concerned about anyone approaching her. He smiled, that curious sensation thumping through his chest once more.

"I am rather undecided if I should appreciate your smile. It seems rather ... devilish."

"It was not meant for you," Theodore said

coolly. "If you will excuse me, Uncle, I have some matters that need my urgent attention."

He stood and walked away, almost bemused by the anticipation filling his chest. There was no reason for her to enjoy the lake alone now, was there?

CHAPTER 3

Chalfont House, Buckinghamshire

Beryl was relieved that her cousins were still abed. She quickly ascended the stairs to her bedchamber, where one of the maids assisted her in changing.

"Thank you, Mary," she said, smiling at the young girl. "You may go now, quickly."

She knew her cousins would berate the kind maid should they ever discover that at times she assisted Beryl. Mary nodded and scampered from the bedchamber. Beryl proceeded to the dining room, where she enjoyed breakfast. She was alone with her meal and thoughts, which kept wandering back to the handsome rogue.

Beryl was breaking the rules again. She could hear her governess, Miss Marsh, telling her, *pride yourself in modesty. You cannot be too circumspect in matters of love and marriage and remember that whereas the character of a young lady is considered angelic, any blemish to it would withdraw the respect men have for you.*

She had taken an unnecessary risk by swimming in the lake. If her cousins had been discovered in the rogue's presence in that state of undress ... Beryl did not want to think about the potential disaster. Her reputation would be in tatters because her cousins would have seen to it. They were malicious and spiteful, and they would not have been able to resist.

The rogue was dashing and he knew it. Overly arrogant and confident. Beryl's skin tingled and she had a premonition ... he was dangerous.

Danger, as in stay away, Beryl.

She would probably ignore her own advice. She wanted to drive him from her thoughts, but she was curious at the same time. There was not much to break up the monotony and despair of her existence. She was upset that he had seen her barely clad and that he did not walk away. He watched her, but for how long? When their gazes had clashed, she felt the heat on her cheeks, and she was sure they were stained bright red. Perhaps she would have gotten to know him if he was not a rake and had they met under different circumstances.

Beryl sighed heavily when she thought of her circumstances. It weighed on her because she could not escape them. As if on cue, her cousins entered the dining room. Lady Edith Ellsworth, Estelle, and Grace. Estelle and Grace were both thin and pale. Neither of her cousins was a great beauty but they were attractive. Grace was the elder sister, and Beryl thought she was particularly spiteful. Beryl had been nothing but kind to them. They told her she would be a companion, but sometimes, she felt like little more than a servant. She had no control over her life and detested the feeling.

How different things could have been if she'd had her season. She was sure she would have received offers, and by now, she would have been married and running her own household.

"You look a bit worse for wear this morning, Beryl," Grace announced as they all took their seats around the dining table.

"I am feeling quite fine, Grace," Beryl replied quietly, wondering what would come next.

"I was not commenting on how you feel but rather on how you look," Grace replied with condescension.

Beryl determinedly kept her hurt and frustration hidden inside. Lady Ellsworth and Estelle stared on, yet neither said a word. They could be equally as rude and patronizing as Grace. Beryl did not think she looked any different from any other day. She knew the source of some of their discontent. They were jealous of her because of her beauty. There was no doubt that when they compared themselves to her, they felt that they had fallen short. Her cousins appreciated physical beauty much more than Beryl did. She was not overly concerned with outer beauty because being kind and compassionate was much more important. It was not that Estelle and Grace were unattractive; they could even be described as remarkably pretty, but envy and spite had made them ugly.

"Perhaps it is her threadbare clothes," Estelle replied as she gave Beryl a dismissive glance.

Beryl's clothes were hardly threadbare. Although they were not the latest fashion, she ensured they were maintained as best she could.

"She already costs me quite enough, and I will

not add new clothes to the list of expenses. You are quite fortunate that we felt pity and took you in, or where would you be now?" Lady Ellsworth asked, and not for the first time.

Beryl did not have an answer to Lady Ellsworth's question, and she did not want to think of it. Everything had happened so fast that she barely had enough time to grieve for her father, let alone think about her future. She tried to remain generous and humble. Beryl knew that she could not change their feelings toward her, so the only thing that she could do was protect herself from their miserliness and snide remarks. She did not argue, and she tried to remain inconspicuous.

"I am most grateful for what you have done for me, Lady Ellsworth," Beryl said.

"Hmm," was all the response that Beryl got.

She cast her gaze down and took a sip of her tea. If there was one thing she could say about her cousins, they were not hypocrites. They were as nasty behind her back as they were to her face. Grace's envy caused her to treat Beryl as if she was dull-witted, but nothing could be further from the truth. Her father had retained the services of a governess, and Beryl was well educated. She enjoyed reading, and she read quite widely. Neither Grace nor Estelle was interested in reading, but Beryl read every day and especially enjoyed it before she went to bed. Beryl was jolted from her thoughts when Lady Ellsworth spoke.

"Grace will debut this season in London. Her gowns have already been ordered, and Madame Lena will arrive shortly to ensure they all fit perfectly. Estelle will be with us in London but will not attend the events. You will have your own season all too soon, Estelle."

"I do look forward to it, Mama," Estelle said with a wide smile.

"You will be coming with us, Beryl," Lady Ellsworth said in a matter-of-fact voice.

Beryl's gaze flashed up from her plate. "Me, to London?"

"Yes. You will act as a chaperone to Grace," Lady Ellsworth announced.

Grace cast Beryl a withering glance. Beryl did not know why because she was just as surprised by the news.

Grace's brows were furrowed when she turned her gaze to her mother. "Are you sure about this, Mama? Why can you not be my chaperone?"

"If I am to chaperone you, then I will not be able to enjoy the season. I am sure Beryl is quite capable of carrying out this task. She can show her gratitude for my generosity," Lady Ellsworth said pointedly.

Beryl wondered if there would ever be a day that they did not remind her of how she came to be at Chalfont House.

"Now, Beryl, you are a young lady in society, so I need not explain the importance of being a chaperone. This will be your primary duty while we are in London. Be warned. You are not attending the engagements for your own merriment. Grace is the priority. You are far too old and you have no dowry. Being old and penniless is not attractive. Do you understand?" Lady Ellsworth stared at Beryl and spoke to her as if she was a child.

"I do," Beryl confirmed as she summoned a small smile.

She was not particularly keen to go to London. Riding in town was not quite the same as in the countryside, and she would miss the lake. Yet, instantly, she recognized the possibility. Her heart started to pound, and she clenched her hands into fists in her lap.

All her life, she had intended to have a family and be the lady of her own house. Life had other plans. Now, this opportunity had presented itself quite unexpectedly. It may be her only chance to secure a respectable match, even though she had no dowry. Her prospects were diminished, but she would not give up. She wanted this, and she would give it her best efforts. Beryl felt a spark of optimism she had not felt in a long time.

They had all finished breakfast when the butler announced that Madame Lena had arrived. Grace and Estelle were so excited that they jumped from their seats, pushing back the chairs.

"Girls!" Lady Ellsworth admonished. "Madame Lena will tend to you first, Grace," Lady Ellsworth announced as she stood.

"I would like Beryl to be there when I try on my gowns." Grace lifted her lips into a smile that did not warm her eyes.

"Certainly," Beryl said, although she knew it was not necessary for her to be there. Ever since arriving at Chalfont House, her time was not hers. There would be no point in saying she did not wish to do it.

Beryl stood and followed her cousins from the drawing room. She saw the staff taking several trunks upstairs. Beryl knew that her cousin could afford for her to have a new gown or two. Beryl was certain that if it were Grace or Estelle in her position, she would not have treated them so. She ascended the stairs and followed Grace to her room, where two trunks were already open.

A woman, who Beryl assumed to be Madame Lena, took one of the gowns and placed it on the bed.

"Madame Lena, I am so happy you are finally here," Grace greeted her.

Grace spun around and commanded Beryl, "Help me to undress."

The word *please* had gone amiss.

"Certainly."

Beryl comforted herself. *This will not be forever.* Not if she had anything to say about it. Beryl remembered her good fortune because being Grace's chaperone could not be more fortuitous. It was the perfect time for her to set her plan in motion. When Grace turned her back toward Beryl, she loosened her dress. The gown that Madame Lena laid on the bed was a beautiful pale-yellow silk.

"This gown will be perfect for you, my lady," Madame Lena said, and she helped Grace to dress.

Beryl had to agree. The gown suited Grace well. The gown had gathers around the waist at the back, a beautiful bow, a flowing skirt, and a low neckline. Grace studied herself, and then she held Beryl's gaze in the mirror.

"Is it absolutely gorgeous! Is it not, Beryl?" Grace exclaimed.

"It is a lovely gown, and you look beautiful in it," Beryl replied.

It seemed that Grace only wanted Beryl to be present so that she could make a show of all her finery. Grace wanted to boast, to give herself even more airs and lord it over Beryl. She wondered what the season would bring for her cousin. Grace was neither good natured nor did she have a kind temperament.

Beryl was comfortable and satisfied with who she was. She did not need constant validation from others because she was confident and self-assured. She chose to remain kind, even in the face of their pettiness.

Madame Lena walked around Grace and checked the gown. She nodded in appreciation as no alteration was required. A perfect fit. Beryl spent the rest of her afternoon with Grace, who tried to make her feel insignificant while she put herself on a pedestal. Beryl took it all in stride and kept her expression serene, which irked her cousin.

Grace had tried on all her gowns, and Madame Lena marked the ones that required alterations. When Grace no longer needed her, Beryl decided to go for a walk in the garden. She could do with a spot of fresh air, and the gardens at Chalfont House were quite exceptional.

As Beryl exited the house, she could not help but think of her father. *I miss you, papa.* They had been close, and he doted on her because she was his only child. At times, she found it hard to accept that he was really gone, but those moments did not last for too long. Still, she longed for the days spent at her much-beloved childhood home, Penrose Hall in Cornwall. It was a great pity the mansion and all its surrounding lands were irrevocably tied to a title that could only be inherited by a male heir.

As she walked among the flowers, Beryl wondered what her prospects would be once in town, and how best she could position herself. Perhaps it was a foolish dream to think she could go from being penniless to finding a *beau* with great fortune. It was not as though she had nothing to offer. She was clever and charming and would showcase this when she went to London. Beryl was confident the lucky gentleman would see her kindness and warm heart once he got to know her.

But what if she failed? What would become of her then? She took a deep breath. Beryl was grateful her father saw it fit to educate her. Typically, girls who were educated learned French, drawing, dancing, and music. She had been taught mathematics, history, geography, and Latin. If all else failed, she could be a governess, but it was not what her heart truly desired.

As a governess, she would enter a life of servitude and fall even further from grace. If she was to take this position, she would exorcise herself from the society she was raised in. A governess occupied the unique position of being neither a servant nor a member of the family. It was an in-between world of isolation and loneliness. Furthermore, she would be vulnerable to the unwelcome advances of men, and she desperately hoped she would never have to live this experience. To make matters worse, many governesses were not paid at all for they should be grateful to have a roof over their heads and three square meals. Those who were paid received nothing but a pittance.

Then there was retirement to plan for, but how would this be achieved on such a measly salary. A good situation and a good employer would allow her to save for her retirement, with provisions for days off, and quarters that were at least better than the servants' living and dining privileges. If the children were girls, she would expect to accompany them on social outings and balls.

Beryl sighed. Although being a governess was perfectly respectable, it would secure her a diminished status and reduce her chances of being the lady of her own home. It was more likely that she would never marry well or have a family of her own.

I must fight for what I truly want. I cannot give up, even in my thoughts.

She wanted a husband and children she would love just as much as her father loved her. She could imagine cradling a tiny infant who she would love unconditionally, who would bring structure, purpose, and direction to her life. She did not want to give up on her dream just yet. It was crushing her soul just to think about what she would lose.

Beryl did not have her head in the clouds. She knew that without a dowry her prospects were limited, but she was not prepared to give up. Not just yet. She was beautiful, cultured and educated. Perhaps her fortunes could be reversed if she managed to capture the imagination of an eligible bachelor of some standing. Surely, she could get a gentleman to fall in love with her. *How hard could it be?* She would not accept defeat until she exhausted all possibilities. She must believe in her capabilities because her future depended on it.

CHAPTER 4

※

Bowden Park, Buckinghamshire

Theodore had awakened several minutes ago but did not leave his bed. He was stretched out atop his sheets, listening to the birds singing outside his window. He took a slow breath deep into his lungs, closed his eyes and listened to their sweet sound.

He was not soothed, and that perplexing sensation pricked at his chest once again. It had been a few days since Theodore's uncle visited Bowden Park. He found that he was restless, so what better way to relieve the feeling than fencing? By the very nature of the sport, fencing was about keeping calm and acting correctly in a quickly changing, physically demanding situation. Theodore excelled at it, for he was reliably cool-headed, and was in good physical form. He had gotten better with practice, persistence, and patience.

He had gone to his friend, Lord Claude Graham, for a match, and they had exhausted themselves. However, Theodore was still restless, and he could not explain why. He wondered if it was because his uncle's words intruded on his consciousness from time to time. Particularly his barb about William turning in his grave.

Bloody hell!

He rang for his valet and with his aid dressed in his riding clothes, and went to the stables. His horse was always prepared because the stable boy knew his routine. An early morning ride was quite invigorating. Theodore set out, and he knew exactly where he would go. The lake. He wondered if he would see her this morning. She would most certainly not be in the same state as when he saw her last. Theodore chuckled as he led his horse into a trot.

The air was fresh and cool. The grass was covered in dew, which brightened with the first rays of the sun. When he entered the clearing, he led his horse into a gallop, the wind rushing by his ears. Sometime later, he slowed his horse and led him down the path, through the copse of trees and into the clearing.

There she is. Theodore inhaled sharply. *She is an enchanting beauty, even though regrettably she is fully clothed.* A wry smile touched his mouth; if she knew his thoughts, the lady would perhaps plant him a facer.

She was perched on a rock close to the lake's shore. Her back was turned to him, so she did not see him approach. A horse was tethered nearby. She was staring at the lake as if the trees that were reflected on the surface held the answer to some mythical question. As he urged his horse forward, he wondered what preoccupied her. Theodore called out because she was deep in thought, and he did not wish to startle her.

"Good morning, my lady," he greeted her with a warm smile as he rode closer to her.

She spun around, and he observed the stiffening in her posture, but she remained seated. At least she did not run away.

"Good morning, good sir," she replied, but her voice held no warmth.

Theodore quickly dismounted and secured his horse. Her hair tumbled carelessly over her shoulders and back in lovely waves. She pushed a few tendrils behind her ear, and he wished that he was able to do it. He wanted to touch the soft silky curls.

"I owe you an apology, my lady."

She said nothing as he advanced, but rather, she scrutinized him with a closed-lip smile. He tried not to stare at her temptingly curved mouth. He stood at a respectable distance, and this time, he could see her lovely blue eyes. They unblinkingly held his gaze. Her facial bones were delicately carved, and she had a seductive young body and fine shapely hips. A sweeping attraction pierced Theodore, but he dared not show it.

She lifted her chin. "For what are you tendering an apology, sir?" There was a mocking lilt to her tone, and her eyes burned with awareness.

Theodore cleared his throat. "I wish to apologize for sneaking up on you when we last met. It was not my intention to spy on you, and I should have announced myself earlier in much the same way that I did today."

He was indeed contrite and hoped it was communicated. Silence hung heavy in the air, and Theodore realized he was holding his breath. He had expected her to accept his apology straight away, but she did not. Their gazes clashed before her stare traveled over the full length of his body. He thought the lady's regard lingered for a moment too long on his chest. Perhaps he imagined it.

"I accept your apology, good sir," she said.

He held her with his eyes, and she did not look away. Theodore saw the redness creep up her cheeks before she dropped her gaze.

Interesting.

She was aware of him just as much as he was of her. The tension curled low in his belly. Could this be the start of a delightful encounter? He fervently prayed it was.

The beginning of a smile tipped the corner of his mouth. "I did not introduce myself. I am Viscount Bowden, and I live on the neighboring property, Bowden Park."

She inclined her head. "I am pleased to meet you, my lord. I am Lady Beryl Keene from Chalfont House."

"Ahh. You are a guest of Lady Ellsworth?" Theodore asked.

"She is my cousin," Lady Beryl replied somewhat reluctantly.

Theodore surmised the lady was probably annoyed that he had interrupted her moment of solitude. He did not wish to leave. Somehow, he felt curious about her. He would stay, although the conversation thus far was much like pulling teeth.

He pretended not to notice, and with as much enthusiasm as he could muster, he said, "I see that you enjoy the lake, Lady Beryl."

She flashed a genuine smile for the first time, and her face lit up. Theodore's heart squeezed. He was fixated on the most sensual, kissable lips he had ever seen. He should not let his gaze linger for too long, for he did not wish to rile her. This was the first time she looked at him as if she did not wish he would disappear, and he enjoyed it.

Lady Beryl glanced at the lake. "The lake gives me great pleasure. I am an early riser, and I find riding quite refreshing. My journey always takes me to the lake. The tranquility and comfort lure me here, and I cannot resist."

He smiled and took a few steps closer. "We share something in common, my lady. Our appreciation for the lake's natural beauty."

"On that, we agree," Lady Beryl said.

Was she pointedly suggesting they would agree on little else?

"I am acquainted with Lady Ellsworth and her daughters. Are you visiting?"

"No, my lord. Chalfont House is my home now."

A shadow of sadness crossed her features before she quickly regained her composure. Now, Theodore was even more curious, but he would not push.

"I am sorry. I did not mean to pry into your private affairs." His words were kind, and he hoped they soothed her. He did not know why he even cared, but somehow, he did not want her to think that he was insensitive. He could not fathom why what she thought of him was of any significance.

"There is nothing to apologize for, Lord Bowden." A forlorn expression covered her face. "My home was Penrose Hall in Cornwall. My father passed away, so I moved to Chalfont House to be with my cousins."

She had put it delicately, but immediately he understood. The laws of succession made no allowances for women. Theodore felt sympathy for her. Surely, this would be a crushing blow for anyone. She had lost her father and her home in short order.

"My condolences." It sounded hollow, but he felt compelled to say it anyway. Theodore walked over to a log and sat down. He looked out onto the lake and decided to share with her. "I have known my share of loss. My parents and, more recently, my brother and his wife. I wish I could offer some words of comfort, that would ease your pain." They were not just empty words. He meant it.

She inhaled audibly. "We are strangers."

Why would you care, her gaze seemed to demand.

"I will say the emptiness and pain you feel will ease in time. Not fully, but I think feeling even the smallest echoes of grief will remind us of those we loved."

She canted her head to the side and gazed at him beneath her lashes for several beats. "I am sorry for your losses, my lord."

Although she did not know him, there was compassion in her voice. He did not mistake it. It warmed him all over.

"Permit me to ask about your mother, Lady Beryl."

The light in her eyes faded. "My mother died when I was very young. I do not remember her," she said wistfully, looking out toward the lake.

She had lost so much for someone so young. Theodore sensed her forlornness deeply, understanding in that moment it might have been her loneliness that prevented her from asking him to leave. She was likely speaking to him because she wanted to feel connected. Perhaps she had not fully adjusted to living with her cousins.

"Were you close to your father?" Theodore asked, hoping that conversation would help her ease some of her sorrows. He owed this lady nothing, but Theodore recalled having no one to speak to about his brother's passing. The hollowness inside had grown until he felt … empty.

The corners of her mouth lifted in a small smile. "I was. Papa was quite attentive, protective, and affectionate. I am grateful for the time I had with him. What about you, my lord?"

Theodore picked up a stone and skipped it over the lake surface. "My brother was the same, protective and loving. When we were younger, I was a bit jealous of him."

"Jealous!"

A wry smile curved his mouth. "William was the favorite, or so I believed. He was the heir and I was the spare. He was to inherit the estate, and he was groomed for it. Then, William got married and had two beautiful daughters. When he passed away, I was charged with caring for them."

"You miss him; I can hear it in your voice."

"Dreadfully," he said gruffly. "I think about him

every day." Theodore's heart lurched, and a sense of bemusement filled him. Why was he sharing such intimate details with her? She was not in his inner circle. Theodore had no immediate answer. Strangely, it was easy to converse with her, almost as if he had known her all his life.

How remarkable.

She turned toward him, and when their gazes locked, frozen in an intimate moment, she quickly looked back at the lake. Her lashes fanned her cheeks, and he thought how alluring they were. He ran his hand through his hair.

Bloody hell. He must stop staring at her so intently lest he frighten her away.

"How old are the children?" she asked, breaking the spell.

Theodore skipped another stone on the water. "Five and seven. Louise recently lost her front tooth, and Mattie follows her big sister everywhere she goes. They remind me of William and I when we were that age."

He felt a thickness in his throat that his brother did not live to see these milestones. He missed William, but he supposed the intense longing would lessen over time. Did they not say that time is the healer of all necessary evils?

"They sound adorable." She sighed softly. "I did not have any siblings, and when I was younger, I wished I did. As I got older, with no brother or sister in sight, I embraced the solitude. Fortunately, you have support in caring for them."

"Support?" Theodore asked.

"Your wife," Lady Beryl replied.

Theodore flashed her a charming smile. "I am not married, Lady Beryl."

Her delicate lips formed an "O," and he could not tear his gaze away from their lush fullness. He wondered what it would be like to taste those lips. He wanted to. Badly.

She was gazing at him, staring at his lips before quickly looking away.

"Will I see you at the lake every day?" he asked. Something unknown inside of Theodore warned him that he would visit daily just to see her.

Lady Beryl's cheeks flushed, and she stared at him with slightly widened eyes. "I will be going to London this season."

He stilled. "You are entering the marriage mart?"

A wary look entered her eyes. "My role is to act as a chaperone for my cousin, who will have her debut."

He carefully observed the nuance of her expression. "Will this be your first foray into society?"

"Though I greatly anticipated having a season, I did not have one because I did not want to leave my father when he was ill."

Theodore liked that she was compassionate. He paused. Why did it matter anyway? If he aimed to bed her, he should not give a fig if she was compassionate. He raked his fingers through his hair, wondering what he truly wanted from Lady Beryl. Theodore discreetly assessed her. He was a good judge of age, and he believed that Lady Beryl was past the age when most young ladies of the *haut ton* would be married or at least be spoken for.

She caught him staring at her, and this time, he was the one who looked away. "You will get the chance to see what you have missed. London is vibrant during the season, and there will be much to do and see."

Lady Beryl gave him a pointed gaze. "Now that you have your nieces to care for, are you going to London to seek a wife?"

Theodore coughed. She had taken him by surprise. It was undeniably direct. She was not afraid to ask. Apparently, she was a woman who knew what she wanted. What else was there? He wanted to know more.

Who are you really, Lady Beryl?

Theodore's thoughts switched to his own character. He was a bit of a rogue. He owned the title and enjoyed debauchery but could never be accused of being a liar. In all his dalliances, he was careful not to lead the ladies to believe he wanted more than he could give. He took pains to ensure he was not to be caught in a compromising position. Some ladies were quite creative in their quest to reach the altar. There would be no scandal that could lead to a forced marriage. He would surely resent being trapped with a scheming wife.

"I do not wish to marry," Theodore said decisively.

Lady Beryl immediately stood up and walked to the water's edge, effectively hiding her expression. He hoped it was not one of disgust, although it would make no difference if it were.

At least a minute passed before she spoke. "Not marry? How extraordinary. Have you always felt that way?"

Lady Beryl bent to collect a few pebbles, stood, and threw each into the lake. She bent, repeating her actions a few times. Theodore's gaze was drawn to her derriere, although he could not see much through all the layers of fabric. He imagined he could. She had a small waist, so he imagined wide hips and shapely legs. A prick of heat rushed through his body.

"Never say it is I who have now stolen your ability to speak?" she drawled.

He wrenched his mind from her shapely figure back to her questions. "I never felt the overwhelming need to marry. My brother was tasked with providing heirs and protecting the title and inheritance. I just wanted to enjoy my life."

"I see," she said softly.

She had moved away from him, but Theodore wanted her to be closer. He cleared his throat. "Would you like to walk along the shore, Lady Beryl?"

"Yes," she said, tossing him a small smile over her shoulder.

Theodore stood up and joined her. They walked in companionable silence for a moment.

"You mentioned looking forward to your season, so I gather you wanted to marry," Theodore said.

"I did." She glanced at him furtively under her lashes.

"Did?" Theodore asked. This was what young ladies of standing were prepared for. They were groomed to provide a suitable match. He recalled then that her role in the upcoming season would be of a chaperone. Was that by choice?

She sighed. "I say *did* because my circumstances have changed. I still wish to marry, but I do not know what the future holds for me."

A few stones, logs and other debris made the path along the shore narrower. Theodore had to move closer to her to allow them to continue walking side by side unimpeded. Their shoulders and arms touched, and he was sure he felt her body heat through their clothing. His skin tingled as if there was no barrier between them. Lady Beryl stopped abruptly, and Theodore turned to face her. The air around them stilled. Her face was feminine and well-modeled. She had big, trusting eyes with thick black lashes, and her nose was exquisitely dainty.

Lady Beryl's tongue darted out and licked her lips. Theodore swallowed, but there was still a lump in his throat. He stepped forward to close the distance between them. She did not step away from him. Her scent drifted toward him, flowers, and soft summer days. Time stood still as they gazed into each other's eyes; hers were compelling and magnetic. His heart beat loudly in his chest, and Theodore was sure Lady Beryl could hear it. There was a charming flush to her cheeks when he fixed his gaze on her lips.

Theodore cupped her jaw, and his mouth swiftly covered hers in a demanding kiss, moving his lips over hers with sensual force. Lady Beryl was left open-mouthed, which was perfect. That was exactly what he wanted, and he took full advantage of it. His lips and tongue explored her as he demanded and cajoled. Lady Beryl gasped, and Theodore felt his heart thump even louder. Her taste was exquisite, and her scent filled his senses. Lady Beryl began kissing him back, mirroring his every stroke. She moaned softly and sighed when he pulled her tightly to him. His breath was ragged; the kiss assaulted his senses in such an intense way. He liked it.

Theodore's hands were entangled in her hair, and the feel of her tresses heightened his need. His tongue traced the delicate softness of her lower lip, and she trembled in his arms. Her lips were warm and welcoming, and he deepened the kiss. The world faded around them, and to kiss her forever would never be long enough. They tasted each other deeply, and still, the kiss went on.

Lady Beryl pulled away. She raised her hand and touched her swollen lips. Her chest was rising and falling, her lush bosom visible over her bodice. Before he could form another thought, Theodore heard the resounding slap across his cheek. The sound reverberated across the lake and among the trees. The burning sensation came afterward. He was so stunned it took him a moment to comprehend what had happened. A woman had never struck him. As the fiery chit raised her hand to deliver another blow, he captured it in a vicelike grip. Theodore lowered his head and brushed her lips tenderly. He released her hand and stepped backward.

Lady Beryl touched her lips with a look of strange wonderment and something more. She had kissed him with such passion and felt the attraction too. Her cheeks were flaming red and her breathing was quick.

"You libertine," she whispered before she spun around and headed back to her horse. She mounted and rode away without a backward glance.

Theodore's breathing was still labored. His face still stung from where she had delivered the blow, and Theodore caressed his cheek. She was right. He was a libertine and he wanted her. Yet, he had his code for whatever it was worth. He would not have her unless she wanted him to. He was sure she slapped him because she was not expecting to be kissed.

Theodore smiled. He enjoyed intimacy and the pursuit of pleasure. He was not ashamed of it. He had a voracious appetite, and he liked to be well-pleasured. Right now, Lady Beryl had his attention. He was forthright and told her he did not wish to marry. This kiss would leave Lady Beryl without a doubt as to his intentions. She stirred his blood and he wanted to seduce her. She would not find a husband in him, but perhaps she would accept a lover.

CHAPTER 5

Beryl had never met a gentleman who took such liberties, and he deserved to be slapped. She was flabbergasted when his lips collided with hers. A rush of excitement quickly had replaced her surprise as his lips crushed hers. His tongue had sent shivers of desire racing through her when it traced her lips. She felt a heady sensation that she had never experienced. His moist, firm mouth demanded a response, and she gave it. Why did he taste so good? The feel of his hand through her hair was so … sensual. Beryl's breath quickened even as she relived the assault on her senses.

Beryl had not thought much about being kissed. She presumed her first kiss would be her intended, the gentleman who would claim her hand. How could she have behaved so inexcusably reckless? If her governess, Miss Marsh, could see her now, she would be discomfited. Miss Marsh always said the rules were there for a reason. One of Miss Marsh's famous rules was not to permit any great intimacies with *any* gentleman. Yet, Beryl had twice been alone with the viscount. What was even more appalling was that he assumed she wanted to be kissed. She had allowed him to kiss her, and she kissed him back. The fact that the kiss stirred something within her was beside the point. He was forward and she encouraged him.

She remembered the feeling of his breath caressing her skin when he swooped in for the second kiss. He exuded danger and she was no fool. Beryl knew he wanted much more than a kiss, yet he made it very clear that he had no plans to marry. Surely, he did not expect her to ruin her reputation by becoming his mistress. Her prospects may be dismal, but she would not countenance an affair.

The libertine!

Beryl enjoyed their conversation, and at the time she was prepared to forget his first misstep. The viscount had to act the fool and ruin it by kissing her. After all, kissing was much more presumptuous than spying. Was it not? Beryl would hardly be able to forget about the viscount. It was her first kiss, and she enjoyed it, but she would not return to the lake. She could not afford to be compromised. Since the viscount frequented the lake, she would find somewhere else to go.

She pushed the viscount from her thoughts. The only thing that should demand her attention now was the upcoming season and how to use this opportunity to her advantage and find the perfect husband!

Ellsworth town house, London
One week later

BERYL HAD SPENT the last few days preparing for the trip to London. Her cousin had sent word ahead, and the servants had been busy preparing the town house in anticipation of their arrival. Beryl had only gone riding on a few occasions. She was relieved not to encounter the viscount even though he haunted her thoughts. Especially in her dreams, she often recalled the softness of his lips and the way he tasted. She tried ardently not to think of the viscount once she was wake, but she did.

How infuriating.

Now she was in town with her cousins, and Beryl hoped she did not encounter the viscount. Given that he was not seeking a wife, perhaps he would be absent from the season. When they arrived in London only a couple days ago, invitations were waiting, and her cousins could not be happier.

They huddled together, discussing the various events, and they pretended Beryl was not in residence. She took advantage of the festive mood and asked Lady Ellsworth if her dear friend, Lady Flora Ely, could visit her. Flora was married and well-connected, so Lady Ellsworth had no cause for concern. She agreed, and Beryl looked forward to spending time with Flora, who genuinely cared for her welfare. She had not seen Flora since she left Cornwall, and there was so much to catch up on.

Her cousins had gone for a carriage ride in Hyde Park. Beryl was reading a book in the drawing room when the butler announced that Flora had arrived. He ushered Flora into the room, and Beryl stood to greet her.

"Oh, Flora, it is so lovely to see you." Beryl hugged Flora.

Flora gave her a reassuring squeeze. "Beryl, I

could hardly wait."

They sat on the sofa close to the window where they could look out into the garden. The sunshine made the flowers even prettier.

Flora reached for her hand. "Beryl, I missed you so much. How have you been?"

"Flora, you have no idea how much I missed you." Beryl was sure to lower her tone. "I did not know what to expect as I did not know my cousins very well. Truth be told, Flora, I am not happy, and I wish that I could be home at Penrose Hall."

"Beryl, I am so sorry. I wish that you never had to leave." Flora's voice was filled with empathy.

Beryl's eyes shimmered with tears, but she blinked them away furiously. "It still hurts when I remember how the new heir of Penrose Hall was smug and condescending in his letter. He acted as if it was I who was trespassing in his home when he was the stranger who had taken over what should rightly be my inheritance."

Flora squeezed her hand comfortingly. "It is so unjust. The things that we women must bear. Sometimes, I fear it is too much. Whatever is the matter at Chalfont House? Please, tell me."

Beryl sighed heavily. "I do not feel the love of my cousins, and I am constantly reminded of what a burden I am. I am not treated much better than a servant. I am grateful that they took me in, but I just wish things were different."

Flora sighed. "You had quite a lot to adjust to with your father passing away, Beryl. You barely had time to grieve."

Beryl shook her head as she expressed her regret. "Sadly, I did not marry, so I am at the mercy of my cousins."

"How awful. At least you are in London, and we will be able to see each other."

"I will enjoy that, Flora." Beryl had always shared her secrets with Flora and knew they were safe with her. "There is something else that I need to tell you."

Flora knitted her brow. "That sounds rather ominous. I hope that you are not ill."

"It is nothing of the sort." Beryl paused and regarded Flora carefully before she spoke. "I met a gentleman."

Flora leaned forward. "You did what? Where? When? Do not keep me in suspense, Beryl."

Beryl relayed the tale up until the viscount kissed her. Flora could not hide her shock, but Beryl reassured her that she had managed to avoid the viscount after their first encounter.

"It is a pity that the viscount turned out to be such a cad. He is young, wealthy, and handsome. He would have made the perfect husband if he was the marrying kind. You have had the most dreadful time, Beryl. Perhaps we should do something to lighten your mood and have a bit of fun." Flora gazed at Beryl expectantly.

Beryl arched a brow. "Fun?"

Flora was daring, and Beryl wondered what she had in mind.

"Why, yes. Lady Oakley is having her famous masquerade ball. It is not the sort of place for delicate ladies, so I doubt your cousin will attend," Flora announced, a twinkle in her eyes.

Beryl gasped. "If it is not a place for young ladies, should we even be going there?"

"Come on, Beryl. My husband is in Wales tending to business, and he will join me here when it is concluded. I have always wanted to go to one of Lady Oakley's famous masquerade balls, and this would be the perfect time."

Beryl's heart pounded. "I am uncertain about this, Flora."

"You could use a bit of a distraction." Her friend was trying hard to convince her.

She thought about it for a moment. "What do

you know of it?"

Flora's eyes lit up. "Mystery and intrigue are the themes of this masquerade ball. We will wear elaborate masks so no one will recognize us. We would certainly enjoy the ball, and you can forget about your worries, even if it is only for one night. What are the chances you will get to enjoy any of the season's balls if you are acting as a chaperone to your spiteful cousin?"

Beryl was warming up to the idea. It had been so long since she had done anything adventurous. "I suppose I could sneak out."

Flora gave her a wide grin. "We will. Mama has a whole host of masks. I only came across them when one of the staff was cleaning the town house, and I peeked into the boxes. I have the perfect one for you, but I will not tell you what it is. You will have to wait and see."

"Oh, Flora. Will you not give me a hint?"

Flora could hardly contain her excitement. "It will be a surprise. Just think about the possibilities. Wearing a mask frees us to do and say whatever we like without worrying about being criticized."

Beryl nodded. "I suppose that is true. Where shall we meet?"

"If you use the back entrance from your garden,

I will be waiting for you with my carriage," Flora announced.

"Unless they are at a ball, my cousins are normally in bed by eight," Beryl said.

"Excellent. I will call for you at nine," Flora replied.

Later that night, Beryl snuck out through the back door and waited in the garden for a few minutes before Flora arrived. Her heart was pounding in her chest, and she was unsure if it was from fear of being caught or from excitement. She wore one of her finest gowns, even if it was outdated. When Beryl recognized Flora's carriage, she opened the gate and exited onto the cobbled street. She entered the carriage and sat across from Flora, and the carriage rumbled on its journey.

Beryl's mouth dropped open as she saw Flora, who was bubbling with excitement. Flora was dressed as a pirate, complete with a hat, beard, and mustache. She even had a spyglass dangling on a strap placed around her neck. Flora was almost unrecognizable.

Beryl raised her brows. "I was not expecting a pirate, Flora."

Flora gave a mischievous grin. "Whyever not?"

Beryl grinned. "I supposed I thought you would

be something more ladylike. A Grecian goddess, perhaps."

Flora gave Beryl a playful look. "What would be the fun in that?"

Flora and Beryl laughed.

"Look what I have for you, Beryl," Flora said as she opened a box that was resting beside her on the seat. Flora opened the box and took out a mask.

Beryl stared wide-eyed at the elaborate mask that would cover her entire face. It was the face of an owl with a fair number of feathers that would help to disguise her hair. She wondered if the feathers were not too long and if she would look ridiculous in the contraption. It was strange yet pleasing.

"I must say, it is beautifully crafted," Beryl said in appreciation. It had taken a great level of skill to produce such detail.

"I knew you would love it," Flora said excitedly as she moved to Beryl's side of the carriage. "Let me help you to put it on."

Beryl felt a surge of anticipation as Flora placed the mask over her face. She reached her hand up to ensure the mask was firmly in place. Flora removed a small mirror from the box, and Beryl stared at her reflection. She was dubious at first, but the mask certainly concealed her identity, and she was pleased with the result.

Beryl took a long, deep breath. "Flora, are you quite certain we will be admitted?" It would be a shame if all their preparation were in vain.

Flora squeezed her hand reassuringly. "I am sure of it. You will soon see because we are almost there."

The carriage came to a stop and they exited. Beryl lost half of her courage when they stood at the entrance of the town house, but it was too late to turn back now. Flora led the way, and they were ushered into a large drawing room.

Beryl gasped. What an impressive sight. She was assailed by the flamboyance and the richly decorated costumes. There were Spaniards, Turks, chimney sweepers, watchmen, conjurers, maids, shepherdesses, gypsies, and sultans. Her eyes flickered from mask to costume, and the attendees were indeed anonymous, for she did not recognize anyone. Beryl thought she had seen it all until a wizard and the devil, complete with a pitchfork, walked toward her and Flora.

Good heavens!

It would be an understatement to say the ball defied the social norm for genteel young ladies. This was a gathering where a lady could be anyone she wanted to be. The thrill of attending an illicit gathering ran through her.

Beryl turned to Flora, whose eyes danced with merriment. She was equally enthralled. "I thought sustaining a character for an entire evening would be impossible. What do you think? It must be difficult to have a ready repartee, in keeping with the character."

"Well, one only needs to be masked until midnight, and then it can be removed," Flora announced.

"But we cannot. We must leave before it turns midnight. It is far too risky," Beryl whispered.

"Fear not, Beryl. We shall. I aim to have some fun, not face ruin," Flora said.

The guests milled around and mingled until the symphony played a lively interlude. The Grecian goddess walked over and claimed Flora's hand for a dance, and Beryl was left alone. Beryl recalled another one of Miss Marsh's rules. No two ladies should dance together without the permission of the host. It hardly mattered because no one could tell Flora was a lady. At this point, Beryl did not think that anyone would care. The usual rules did not apply here.

Beryl wandered out of the drawing room, intending to find the refreshment room. She walked down the hallway, where the music faded and grew quieter. She entered a room on the right with many coats and cloaks, some neatly hanging while a few were carelessly draped over the chairs. She needed to exit and continued down the hall. It would probably be the next room. Beryl was just about to turn around when she heard whispers from an adjoining room. The door was slightly ajar, and she had not noticed it. The voices drifted toward Beryl.

"I have removed my mask," the lady said with a flirtatious voice.

"Hmm, I can see that," the gentleman replied.

The flirtatious tone convinced Beryl that she had come across a private moment. She should leave and give the couple their privacy, but she was far too curious. Who was the lady who had unmasked herself? There would be no harm in finding out, provided she remained concealed. Beryl quietly moved toward the door and peered through the crack. She could see the gentleman and lady standing close to each other. Quite close. They were intimate. She saw their side profile, and in the dimly lit room, she did not recognize the lady.

"Did I tell you how ravishing you look in that

dress," the gentleman smiled as he threw his arm around her waist, lowered his head, and kissed her.

Beryl's heart skipped. She had never come across a couple doing anything untoward before. The lady appeared to enjoy being kissed because she sighed, and he groaned. Beryl's heart beat faster as she remembered how much she enjoyed her first kiss with the viscount. She did not want to be caught eavesdropping, yet her inquisitiveness outweighed her better judgement. She stood rooted in the spot.

The lady broke the kiss and pulled away. "We must stop before someone wanders in."

"Is it not all the more exciting this way? The thrill?" he asked as he leaned down and nibbled her ear.

The lady gasped.

Beryl thought the gentleman was intoxicated. He reminded her of her father when he had one too many whiskeys. The gentleman must be foxed to think that a lady would want to be caught in a compromising position. He moved from kissing her ear to her cheek.

"You are such an angel," he whispered as he planted little kisses all over her face and bosom with a strange kind of eagerness.

The lady struggled to get away from him. "Not here, darling," she pleaded.

The gentleman sighed in frustration. "If that is what you want," he petulantly replied.

"It is," she said as she replaced her mask.

Oh dear. The couple were about to leave, so Beryl spun around and hurriedly exited the room. Her heart thudded in her chest. She went directly to the drawing room where the dance had just ended, and the symphony played an interlude. It was only when she arrived that she remembered her refreshment. She had not found the room, and she was rather thirsty. She decided to wait until Flora reappeared, and they could go together. Beryl felt hot and flustered under her mask, but she dared not remove it. Perhaps later, she could take a turn in the garden.

The symphony played on, and rather suddenly, Beryl became aware of another presence beside her. She turned and came face to face with the wizard. It was the very same wizard who was walking with the devil earlier. He was not the typical older man with a long beard; rather, he was tall and imposing, and the wizard's hat made him appear even more so. He was wearing a black half-mask, and her eyes dropped to his mouth. It must be because it was exposed. When she lifted her gaze, he was staring at her intently. She flushed and felt the warmth on her cheeks.

"May I have the next set, my lady?" The wizard's smooth voice flowed to her ears. He held out his arm to her.

Beryl sucked in her breath. There was something familiar about him, but she could not put her finger on it. The corners of his lips lifted in a wicked smile, and his head tilted to the side expectantly. Slowly she exhaled.

"We have not been introduced, but the rules are always altered here. We can remain anonymous," he drawled, his eyes twinkling with humor.

"Well, in that case, I am Owl, and you are Wizard," Beryl replied, wondering why Flora had not reappeared after the last set. She placed her hand in his own.

As he led her to the dance floor, Beryl wondered if they had ever met. She was trying quite hard to remember, which was rather annoying because she could not place him. Surely, that was the point of the mask. His gaze was mesmerizing as the wizard held her in position for the dance. Beryl wondered if he would wield his magic and cast a spell on her tonight.

CHAPTER 6

Theodore recognized her voice instantly. It is not every day that one comes across a lady swimming in a lake, much less one that could deliver such a slap.

When he walked by, he heard her speak to her companion, the pirate. He had excused himself from the mundane conversation he was having to go in search of her, only to see her disappear down the hall. He followed her but hung back when she suddenly stopped in the cloakroom. He approached the cloakroom door cautiously and peered inside. He quietly smiled when she tiptoed toward another door and peered through the crack; so much for accusing him of spying. He quickly turned away and returned to the ballroom, chuckling under his breath. Theodore had patiently waited for her to resurface.

Theodore enjoyed dancing. He placed an arm at the small of her back, and she placed an arm on his shoulder. He liked the feel of her hands on him. His eyes dropped to her lips. How could he forget moving his mouth over hers with carnal persuasion and her soft whimper. What he would do to have his tongue intertwined with hers again.

"Your mask serves you well, Owl; you cannot be easily recognized," he said as the symphony started up.

He could imagine gently removing her mask and ravishing her with sensuous kisses. He was grateful for the opportunity to hold her, and even the light feel of her hand aroused him.

"I believe that is the point, Wizard," she said.

The mask did not hide her beauty entirely. As they swept across the floor, he said, "The style and quality of your mask says something about the lady wearing it. You have only revealed enough to tantalize."

"A wizard who pays compliments. Thank you. Why did you choose to adopt the wizard as your persona?" Her eyes were searching and piercing.

"I wanted to be magical, or should I say

mythical? A wizard is knowledgeable and has explored frontiers others do not know exist." He wanted to explore her mouth even more thoroughly than he did the first time. Would she give in to her sensual desire and let him taste her?

Her lips curved in a smile. "I have often thought of a wizard as one who could make the storms gather and strange sights appear. So, there is an element of magic which makes the wizard more powerful."

"Indeed," he murmured.

Her eyebrows furrowed, and then she released them. "Tell me, are you a good or a naughty wizard?"

His cock jumped at the word naughty. *If only she knew*. Theodore chuckled and raised a brow. He was surprised by the question. "I am neither malevolent, dangerous, nor evil. You are safe with me."

Her eyes lit up and he yearned to know the secrets inside. "Ahh, I suppose that means you are good then."

There was a certain warmth about her that made him think of the warm glow of the sun heating one's skin on a cool day. A small warning sounded in his head. *Bloody hell!* He wondered if he had taken leave of his senses. He was not the poetic sort.

Theodore pondered her comment for a moment. "I would venture to say that not being bad does not mean one is good."

She arched her brow and gave him a quizzical look. "Oh?"

Theodore gazed into her eyes before he quickly looked away. "Although it implies that may be the case, it is not always easy to distinguish someone as simply good or bad."

She wrinkled her perfectly pert nose. "Whatever do you mean? Ambiguity? I find the distinction easy enough to make."

This time, when her eyebrows shot up, their gazes locked. His breath hitched, and his heart beat faster in his chest. Momentarily, he forgot what he was about to say. They glided across the floor, and he was oblivious to everyone around them. She felt so right in his arms, and he enjoyed the set and her company. He wondered how it could be. How could he have had so few encounters with her, yet she dominated his thoughts?

Theodore quickly recovered. "Do you not believe that good people sometimes do bad things? Or even more than one bad thing, for that matter."

She caught her lower lip between her teeth in concentration, and he almost missed what she was saying. "I can appreciate that someone may do something completely out of character. I suppose that is understandable, yet I would have serious reservations about anyone who repeats such actions?" Her eyes studied him before moving to a faraway look.

He wondered if she was thinking of the man she met at the lake. Was she wondering if there was more good than bad in him? He was being ridiculous. Surely, this could not be. Yet, he wondered if when she lay in bed at night she thought about his kiss.

Theodore would admit he was a bit of a rogue, but he would hardly describe himself as *bad*. To his reasoning, it was just that he was not entirely good. Is anyone? He wanted to enjoy his life, for you only live once. He was unapologetic. He did not agree with his uncle, who thought he needed to be reformed. He was perfectly fine the way he was.

"The way I see it, someone bad does something with the intent to cause harm to another person. Whereas a good person may do something bad accidentally, or at the very least does not pride themselves on doing bad things and certainly would not make a habit of it," Theodore said. He was always open and direct in his conversation. He said whatever he wanted without anxiety or concern.

She appeared interested in his commentary.

She raised a brow. "So, you are saying it is a person's intent rather than their actions that makes them bad?"

Theodore felt so comfortable holding her in his arms. It was almost as good as a kiss. "Indeed." He studied her. "You look skeptical. If you do not accept my argument, do you suggest that humankind is selfish and heartless and thrives on engaging in wrongful or illicit deeds?"

Her tongue darted out before she bit the corner of her lip, and he almost missed his step.

Lady Beryl tilted her head to the side. "I am not so pessimistic. Yet, my experiences have taught me that the world is filled with bad people who will never truly be able to appreciate anything or anyone who is goodhearted. They ruin everything that they touch."

Lady Beryl had a story, and he wondered what it was. It would only be natural for her to hide her true feelings in his presence, but she did not. "So cynical for one so young."

She smiled, but it did not touch her eyes. "I may be young, but I fear that I have already lived experiences well beyond my years." Her chin lowered and her hand went limp.

At that moment, Theodore knew the lady was not thinking of him. His hand on the small of her back felt the tension in her body. She had experienced something more profound. He made a clumsy attempt to comfort her but only managed to give her a weak smile. He wished he knew what was causing her such distress, but if she did not share her name, she would be unlikely to share any intimate details. He wished that he could alleviate her pain, but since he could not, he hoped that her circumstances would change.

All too soon, the set ended, and he was intrigued. He must know more about her. Probably, he should not. He already knew that they wanted very different things. A romp versus a marriage. Yet, it had been a long time since a lady so effortlessly captured his attention. He pulled his breath in and slowly released it. They walked away from the dance floor.

"Thank you, Owl. I enjoyed your company."

Theodore bowed. "Would you like some refreshments?"

"Thank you. A glass of wine would be welcomed. It is rather stuffy in this room." She retrieved a small and delicate fan and proceeded to fan herself. It was indeed hot and humid.

Theodore nodded in rapt attention. "Wine it is. I will return momentarily."

As Theodore walked away, his thoughts turned to their kiss by the lake. He recalled the way she had melted into his kiss, the soft feel and taste and the breathy sounds she had made when he captured her lips. Of course, she would never have danced with him if she knew his true identity. Theodore wondered if perhaps this would not be an opportunity for them to start afresh. He knew it was a foolish thought because she did not know who he was, but he felt compelled to spend time with her.

He sensed her vulnerability. Lady Beryl was lonely, a bit lost even. She could not keep the unhappiness from her voice and the combination made her mysterious and complicated, which drew Theodore to her even more. He wanted to peel back layers of the mystery and discover what lay beneath. Theodore returned with the wine and handed her a glass.

Beryl fanned herself but appeared less than pleased with the result.

"It is quite warm. Shall we take a turn in the garden?"

"I welcome a breath of fresh air," she replied.

Guests at these balls had little concern for convention and propriety. He could be alone with her, undisturbed for as long as they wanted. Theodore escorted Lady Beryl through the large patio double doors that led into the garden. He pulled the cool night air into his lungs, and it was a relief from the warm crush.

As they made their way down the cobbled path, Theodore asked, "What is the most wicked thing that you have ever done?"

Lady Beryl's steps faltered before she stopped, turned, and stared at Theodore. He flashed her a devilish grin as he waited for her reply.

A delicate eyebrow arched. "I beg your pardon?"

"You heard me the first time. What is the most wicked thing you have ever done? Only moments ago, you had such interest in whether people were good or bad. I believe you conceded good people can do bad things. So, even if you are a good person it stands to reason you must have done something wicked at some point."

Lady Beryl's light laughter was a rich sound that echoed through the garden. She took a sip of her wine and answered with the most solemn expression. "I killed a spider once."

Laughter floated up from Theodore's throat, and he eyed her with amusement. "A spider?"

"Well, yes. I woke up one night to find it crawling along my arm. It was the most frightening and disgusting thing, so I quickly reached for a book I had fallen asleep with and brushed him from my arm. Sadly, he lost a few legs so I had to put him out of his misery," Lady Beryl explained with a straight face.

They had not resumed walking, and Theodore was admiring her animated expression. He chuckled. "And how old were you when you had this sobering experience?"

Lady Beryl flashed a grin. "I was all of nine years old, and it was quite a traumatic experience. I refused to sleep alone in my room for a few nights, and a maid was assigned to stay with me. I was all grown up by then, and I hated being chaperoned at night as if I was a baby, but my fear of spiders was greater. Of course, father thought I was overreacting."

"Well, when you look back at it, can you blame him?"

"I suppose not, but there are many things that live in the imagination of a nine-year-old." Lady Beryl took another sip of her wine and set off walking in the direction of seats in the garden. The seats were rather small for two people, particularly with his large frame. Theodore would not let that stop him. He would be closer to her. They sat and he took a swig of his drink. Even by his standards they were sitting rather close, their knees touching and his hips were pressed against hers. She did not seem to be bothered. Nobody knew who she was, and people did not come here to have regard for what others were doing. Surely, the mask had given her the anonymity she craved.

"When you are nine years old, insects terrify you, but as an adult, you come to learn that it is our own species that we should fear," Lady Beryl said.

Theodore did not fill the silence that descended around them. He wanted her to reveal more. For a moment they shared a space where sound did not exist, just an inner stillness. Yet, it was not devoid of thought.

"You are saddened," he murmured.

Lady Beryl cast him a quick glance of surprise. "I lost my father within the last year, and it has been the single most painful experience of my life."

"The death of a loved one is always heart-wrenching," Theodore said gruffly, wishing he could do more to soothe her.

Lady Beryl glanced up at him, and he saw the pain in her eyes. She looked away as though to hide her vulnerability and took a sip of wine.

Theodore remembered how he felt when William passed away. Sad, angry, depressed, confused, and at times hopeless. What was the point of being reputable when such a good, favored son was ripped away for no reason? He did not want to admit that he was vulnerable and wanted to protect the most vulnerable parts of himself. He cringed at the thought of exposing his feelings to the world. Protecting those sentiments would keep him safe.

Perhaps his disreputable behavior was protecting him from the emotional pain. He had turned his nose up at many of society's norms and challenged them on a regular basis. He became more impulsive and uninhibited. *Fuck them*! He would do as he damned well pleased. None of them would tell him what to do. As he stood there waiting for Lady Beryl to open up, he acknowledged that the emotional barriers that he set up were to keep the loneliness, unhappiness, and hopelessness at bay. "There is no one about," Theodore murmured. "You can yell, curse, and do whatever you want to get those feelings out."

A shaky laugh escaped her. "I should perhaps scream, shouldn't I? I lost my childhood home, and I am at the mercy of my cousins. I can tell you they are a set of sharks that smell blood in the water. They are prepared to tear the injured to pieces without regret. Such pleasure in inflicting suffering when there is no need for it."

Theodore felt as if he wanted to smash his first into something. The pain in her tone ravaged something unknown inside of him. "Once one is on a path of cruelty, it can be difficult to change one's mind. What do you suppose is the reason for their ill treatment?"

"My diminished circumstances would be my guess. After all, I have no one to stand up for me, no one to protect me now that my father is gone."

"They are being quite cruel to you. How do you think of crushing them?"

"Crushing them?" Lady Beryl asked.

"Yes. Do not tell me you have not fantasized

about it?" Theodore said, as he waited, wondering what she would say.

Lady Beryl lightly laughed. "I suppose I am going about it rather slowly by elevating myself above such behavior. I'm a decent human being, and I will not stoop to this level of cruelty."

In the face of cruelty, Lady Beryl took the high moral ground, and he admired her for it.

"Surely, you fantasize about perhaps putting a bucket of spiders under the sheets when they are asleep in bed. Or centipedes, perhaps?" Theodore asked.

Lady Beryl giggled. "You may think it is a good idea to crush your enemies, but may I remind you that I live among the sharks?"

"I take your point, but I have seen many examples of enemies that have been left alive only to end up returning for revengeful chaos. There is an advantage in crushing your enemies … totally." Theodore said. "Or …"

Beryl raised her glass and finished her wine all the while holding Theodore's gaze. "Or what?"

"I could slay them for you if you would let me."

Her probing gaze caused his heart to pound in his chest.

"I will fight my own battles in my own way,

thank you. I would like to return to the ballroom," Lady Beryl said, standing.

Theodore escorted her inside and as soon as they entered, he saw the pirate approaching, and he could tell by the gait that it was a woman.

"A glass of wine for you, my lady?" Theodore asked.

"Thank you," the pirate replied before reaching up to ensure her hat was secure.

Theodore walked away and rubbed his hands together. He went to the refreshment room to procure the wine, but when he returned to the drawing room the ladies were nowhere to be found.

What the hell!

His scanned the room, searching for an owl and a pirate, but he did not find them. Theodore felt rather foolish standing there staring with two glasses of wine in his hand.

Why the devil had they run off?

CHAPTER 7

Theodore pressed his lips tightly together. He was disappointed because he planned to ask Lady Beryl to dance with him again. He wondered if perhaps she discerned who he was, but he dismissed the notion. That could not be possible in the short time it took to fetch the wine. Theodore did not have time to consider it further. His partner in debauchery was approaching. Howard Carlton, the Duke of Moreland, joined him. He was dressed as the devil and quite enjoyed playing the part. The devil had notoriety even at a masquerade ball.

"There you are, Bowden. I wondered where you disappeared to," Moreland said.

"Would you like a glass of wine?" Theodore asked.

Moreland's gaze flickered between the wine glass and Theodore's face. "There is a story here, Bowden. I know you did not have a glass of wine waiting for the off chance that I would find you." Moreland smirked. "Let's hear it."

Theodore chuckled. He met Moreland at a famous decadent party. On the surface, the *haut ton* was prudish, but he belonged to a set that knew how to enjoy life. They were of the same class, and although they did not discuss it openly, they indulged in behavior those with the stiff upper lip would certainly frown upon.

"I have been jilted," Theodore said sheepishly.

Moreland chuckled and accepted the wine. "*You?* Jilted? This should be interesting. Pray, tell."

Theodore took a sip of his wine. He would tell Moreland about her, but not too much. "I recently met a young lady, and she piqued my interest. We danced, and I went off to fetch the wine, and when I returned, she was gone. I have scanned the room, but it appears she left."

Moreland bit his cheek and scrutinized Theodore's face. "Is that it? I know you, Bowden. I sense there is more to the story, and you have given me the abridged version, so out with it."

Theodore smiled. "I should have known there

was no likelihood of pulling a fast one." He took another sip of his wine, and Moreland waited expectantly. "A few weeks ago, I met a young lady when she was out for a horseback ride in the morning. I must say, we did not get off to a good start. I acted like a bit of a lout. When I saw her the next time, I apologized, but then I behaved like an even bigger lout."

Moreland's wine glass was halfway to his lips, and he paused. "What the devil did you do?"

"I felt the overpowering need to kiss her, and I did," Theodore said.

"And? Do not keep me in suspense." Moreland urged.

"I suppose I shocked her because she slapped me," Theodore said sheepishly.

Moreland gave him a sideway glance of utter disbelief before his mouth quirked with humor.

Theodore sighed. "I am pleased to see that at least I am keeping you entertained."

Moreland chuckled. "Surely, this is the first time a lady slapped you and for kissing at that. After all, your conquests are usually eager to be kissed."

"I put it down to her relative inexperience. Even though she slapped me, I could tell that she enjoyed the kiss." Theodore's thoughts flashed back to her soft lips and her taste when she opened her mouth to him for the first time. Exquisite.

"You know that I have my rules, Moreland. I am not looking for a wife; anyone who comes to my bed is told, and they must come willingly," Theodore said.

"I gather the lady seeks a husband," Moreland replied. "It is the only thing that makes sense."

"Precisely." Theodore was sure Moreland understood how he felt about being trapped in a marriage. He, too, was single and endeavored to avoid a similar fate.

Moreland's eyes widened. "Hang on. And you are telling me that this lady was here tonight, and you recognized her?"

"Yes. I did," Theodore replied.

Moreland raised a brow. "How uncanny? Did she recognize you?"

Theodore waved a hand. "Of course not. She has avoided our meeting place ever since we kissed. I have no doubt she would have refused to dance or even speak to me."

Moreland was hesitant when he spoke, but he was studying Theodore like a hawk. "Well, as per your rules, why do you even want to pay her any more attention? She wants a husband and you want a dalliance. As you well know, these are at odds."

"You are stating the obvious, Moreland." Theodore sipped his wine.

"Yet, you have not answered my question." Moreland chuckled. "Why?"

"For one, she is exceptionally beautiful," Theodore said, although he knew this was not the reason.

Moreland pinned him with a hard stare. "I know you have met beauties across the continent. Many are all too willing to share your bed."

Theodore thought of the first time he saw her in the lake. To think she accused him of being inappropriate when her activities would not be considered appropriate by the society into which she wished to marry. It took gumption to square up to him. "She is bold, direct and honest."

Moreland flashed a wicked grin. "Bold, I can understand. The slap tells me that."

Theodore ran his hand through his hair. "Do not take liberties, Moreland; otherwise, I will be forced to find another partner in crime."

Moreland placed his free hand over his heart and feigned injury. "You have hurt me, Bowden. Things would not be the same without you."

Without any further prompting from Moreland, Theodore said, "She is intelligent, witty and unafraid to speak her mind."

"Hmm. Interesting." Moreland was staring at him intently.

"At the same time, she is mysterious, and I can sense her sadness. There is a part of me that wishes to … take it away from her," Theodore said. Her sadness was palpable, and it gutted him that she endured it.

"Bowden, my good man, it is clear to me that you should avoid this particular lady for obvious reasons. She does not fit your mold, and you may find yourself in an uncomfortable position. Your rules are there for a reason, and they protect you," Moreland carefully explained.

Theodore sighed and shifted his weight from one leg to the other.

Moreland continued, "I say this as your friend. She is innocent and inexperienced, and you should leave well enough alone."

Theodore gave a heavy sigh. "Perhaps you are right."

Even though he largely agreed with Moreland, Theodore wondered when he would see Lady Beryl again. She would attend most social gatherings as a chaperone. He was sure to see her. How will she react when they come face to face?

As Beryl prepared for the Wilford's ball, she could not help but think of the masquerade ball. Flora had lost her nerve when she ran into Lord Henry Newell, and although she was well disguised, she was petrified she would be recognized. Flora's anxiety was infectious, and as soon as the wizard went for refreshments, they left the ball. Beryl had enjoyed the dance with the wizard and the shiver of excitement she felt when she walked through the guests, knowing that no one recognized her. She was not the poor, ill-treated orphan.

There was a knock on her door, and before she could speak, it was opened. Grace stood in the door and demanded, "What are you doing?"

"I am preparing for the Wilford's ball," Beryl replied.

Grace sneered. "You are *my* chaperone, Beryl. You need not take so much care with your appearance. *You* do not need to look perfect; *I* do. You will hardly be noticed in your frumpy, out-of-date gown."

"I see." Beryl fought to maintain her composure because there was no need for such a biting remark.

Grace crossed her arms and gave Beryl a hard squint. "Your time will be better spent assisting me with dressing."

"Is Mildred not assisting you?"

Grace snorted and gave an exaggerated eye roll. "She is, but I want you there. Is that an inconvenience for you? I should hope not, considering all that we have done for you. I hardly think you want Mother to conclude you are ungrateful."

Beryl merely said, "Certainly not, Grace. I will be with you shortly."

"I should hope so." Grace gave her a haughty look before she spun around and left the doorway as quickly as she entered.

Beryl's eyes misted. *Oh, Papa, if ever you could see the indignities I have suffered.* Her heart was aching. She had such a feeling of heaviness and tightness in her chest and limbs. She wished for the umpteenth time that her father was alive, and she was in her childhood home. The tears were threatening to spill over. She drew deep breaths and blinked rapidly. She would not give Grace the satisfaction of appearing with puffy eyes and splotchy skin.

Beryl walked to the dressing table, where she had a pendant containing her father's portrait. She opened it, and a loving face looked back at her. The tears once again threatened, and she closed the pendant and kissed it. Beryl balled her fist around it and held it to her heart as she rocked back and forth on her heels. She sighed heavily, replaced the pendant, and stood staring at her hands. Beryl lifted her chin, squared her shoulders and walked from the room down the hall to Grace's room.

Mildred had already laid out Grace's gown, and it was one of Madame Lena's creations.

Beryl was still in her loose-fitting day dress. They were similarly attired this morning because they were not expecting any callers today. Grace was now wearing a sacque, and Beryl was sure she had already had her bath. Mildred was pinning her hair, which was a mass of black curls.

"What would you like me to do, Grace?"

"See that all my undergarments have been laid out, and my jewelry is polished. I do not believe I found the shoes I would wear with my dress," Grace snapped.

Beryl nodded. "I will see to it."

She walked over to the bed. A corset, a knee-length chemise, and layers of flounced petticoats had been laid out. Beryl assembled and polished Grace's jewelry and selected her shoes. By this time, Mildred had completed pinning Grace's hair. Grace stood up, and Mildred started removing her sacque. Beryl moved forward to accept it and placed it on the bed. She removed the rest of her undergarments, and Beryl handed the fresh pieces to Grace as she called for them.

Beryl could not fathom why she was there. There was nothing here that Mildred could not do, but Beryl knew better than to express her opinion. She attended to her duties with efficiency and watched as Grace admired her reflection in the mirror.

"Madame Lena had certainly outdone herself. This gown is so beautiful; I will be the belle of the ball," Grace boasted.

"It is a lovely gown that suits you well," Beryl replied.

Although they were unkind to her, to say the least, Beryl always remained amiable. She did not have a mean bone in her body. She refused to let their cruel treatment change her nature.

Grace smirked. She continued to preen and stare at her reflection. Suddenly, Grace looked at Beryl. "You should get dressed, Beryl, or we will be late, and I will not be blamed for it." Grace held up both hands and shooed Beryl from the room. "Well, off you go."

Beryl hurried from Grace's room to hers. Lady Ellsworth abhorred tardiness, and Beryl would not be the butt of her derision. She was pleased that she had already prepared everything that she needed and chose a gown that flattered her well. Hilda helped her to dress, but there was no time to make her face more presentable with even a bit of rouge. Rather than being poised, she was flustered as she rushed to meet her cousins at the front door. She was relieved when they departed without any snide remarks.

They sat in the carriage, and as it pulled away, Beryl hoped she would catch the eye of an eligible bachelor. Her future security depended on it. Marriage was the center of everything this evening, and the attachments formed by the season's end would ripple through society.

Beryl sat in the carriage with her cousins and glanced at each of them in turn. There was not one who had her best interest at heart. They were selfish and mean. The thought of being at their mercy forever sent a chill up her spine. She must find a man of means with better social status.

For the first time, Beryl was quite pleased that her cousins talked over her as if she was absent. Her thoughts drowned out their incessant, excited chatter. Beryl wanted children, and she vowed they should never suffer the same fate as her.

The carriage pulled up to the Wilford's town house, and they alighted. They were ushered into an already packed drawing room where the upper echelons of society freely mingled. Beryl was here to find a husband just like all these society belles. She had no dowry, yet she secretly hoped for a kind and decent man. She was sure by the end of the season many of the young ladies would be spoken for. They would not struggle like she would. Despite knowing what she wanted was almost impossible, she resolved not to give up. She had to convince herself of the merits of her plan.

Lady Alberta Truman, the Duchess of Wilford, came over to greet them, and Lady Ellsworth made the necessary introductions.

"Let me introduce you to some of my guests," Lady Wilford said, and she led her cousins away.

Beryl followed through the round of introductions. Grace had been asked to dance, but Beryl had been looked upon as more of a curiosity. The gentlemen of the *haut ton* did not ignore her because she supposed that would be difficult to do. Her beauty and grace were such that she turned heads when she entered a room.

Lady Wilford was just about to take them to meet another set of guests when she peered over Beryl's shoulder. They all turned toward Lady Wilford's gaze and she said, "There you are. May I present Lord Theodore Godwin, Viscount Bowden?"

Beryl stiffened, her muscles rigid, and she was sure her heart stopped. It was inevitable that they would meet, yet she hoped it would not be this soon. Her skin tingled, and there was a fluttering in the pit of her belly. He was just as devilishly handsome as she remembered. He was immaculately garbed in black trousers and jacket, with a blue waistcoat and black cravat. Her gaze fell to his lips before she quickly looked away. She was sure her cheeks were flaming red, for she felt the heat. Lady Wilford had continued with the introductions, and she heard her cousins reply, but it seemed to be from far away.

Beryl felt a slight nudge in her back, and four pairs of eyes looked at her expectantly.

"I am pleased to make your acquaintance, Lord Bowden," Beryl replied mechanically.

"Would you do me the honor of sharing the first dance, Lady Beryl?" His eyes twinkled and held a hint of something more.

There were soft gasps of alarm from her cousins.

The viscount was wicked. He had asked her in the presence of the host, and it would be difficult for her to refuse. Beryl was sure he knew she could not say no. Beryl registered Grace's fierce glare. Lord Bowden had not asked her to dance. This did not bode well for Beryl, and she wondered what Grace and Lady Ellsworth would say when they were alone.

Beryl buried her groan and smiled. "I will reserve the first dance for you, Lord Bowden."

Just then, the orchestra started the interlude for the first dance. Even they were conspiring against her. Beryl thought it was such a waste to dance with him because he was not looking for a wife, and she would not be his mistress. Lord Bowden led her to the dance floor. They took their position, and a few beats later the waltz started.

Her heart lurched when he gracefully led her into the rousing dance.

"You are a beautiful dancer," he murmured, his gaze far too intent upon her.

"I ..." Beryl was almost uncertain what to say.

"Ah, the lady is blushing," Lord Bowden drawled, looking far too pleased.

She delicately sniffed. "It is merely the heat from a far too crowded ballroom."

"A pity, I thought it was due to your reflection of our delightful kisses and being so close to my charm."

The sound that spilled from Beryl was one of shock. The rogue grinned, the curve of his mouth so sensual, wild flutters went off in her belly. "I have not thought about your ... kiss once."

"Pretty little liar."

Their gazes collided. "You cannot be certain," she said, grateful her voice was steady.

"I can, for every day I thought about your mouth against mine."

Her cheeks burned, and she was thankful they finished their dance in silence. There was a secret thrill inside Beryl that he was similarly haunted by their illicit encounter. After their set, Lord Bowden led her back to her cousins. Beryl realized that Grace was not dancing, but before they could start a conversation, she saw Lady Wilford walking purposefully toward them. All heads were turned in Lady Wilford's direction. She escorted quite a dashing young gentleman, and Beryl thought he would surely catch Grace's eyes. Her heart lurched when Lady Wilford stood before her to make the introductions. She quickly cast a glance at Lady Ellsworth, who wore a smile, but her eyes were filled with anger. Beryl recognized the look, and she knew Lady Ellsworth was not happy.

Beryl barely heard the words that were exchanged and dared not glance at Grace when the Earl of Stanmore spoke.

"Lady Beryl, may I have the next dance?"

"Certainly, my lord." Beryl had long decided she would take advantage of every opportunity she got, even if it made her cousins furious.

The earl turned to Grace. "May I reserve the next dance with you, my lady?" He did not address Grace by name and asked her to dance as if it was an afterthought.

"It would be my pleasure, Lord Stanmore," Grace replied with a stiff smile.

Lord Stanmore bowed and led Beryl to the dance floor.

The orchestra started up, and soon, they were twirling and swirling across the floor.

"Is this your first season, Lady Beryl?" Lord

Stanmore asked. His eyes seemed to be on Beryl's cleavage.

"It is, my lord," Beryl replied.

Lord Stanmore finally gazed at her face and raised a brow. "A bit late, is it not?"

Beryl drew in a sharp breath. She was not expecting such a direct question, for they had only just been introduced. His familiarity was off-putting.

"Family commitments waylaid me, Lord Stanmore," Beryl said.

"I see," he said, although Beryl knew he did not. He could not know. "I am certain I would have remembered such remarkable beauty." The compliment seemed hollow.

They twirled across the dance floor among the other graceful couples.

"Thank you, Lord Stanmore."

"Although we have not met, I know of your father. Such a sorry state of affairs after his demise," he said with a sniff, implying distaste.

Beryl thought he did not sound sorry but rather perfunctory. She cleared her throat. "We all deal with death at some point in life, Lord Stanmore."

Although Beryl had employed some diplomacy, it fell on Lord Stanmore's deaf ear. "It is not only that he died, but it is the sorry state that he left you in."

Beryl felt herself stiffen. She wondered why the earl was being so rude. He was certainly arrogant. That may be putting it lightly. *Insufferable*.

Beryl felt the need to defend her father. "My father wanted me to have a season, Lord Stanmore. It was I who delayed it to be with him at the end."

"How dutiful and admirable. So, you still wish to find a husband, do you?"

He may not have said the words, but his tone did. He was reminding Beryl she had limited prospects, and it hung in the air between them. Beryl wondered why Lord Stanmore would ask her to dance and behave in such an ungentlemanly way. He had no genuine interest in her if he was being so crass, surely? Beryl decided she would not stoop to his level. Whether she was seeking a husband or not was none of his damned business.

"I am here as a chaperone for my cousin, but I will keep an open mind." Beryl would at least be polite, although she did not feel like it.

Lord Stanmore stared at her with a smug smile. "You have been groomed for marriage but will not achieve it. I am a wealthy man, and I can provide you with property, perhaps in St. John's Wood, servants, a new wardrobe, and an income. You would want for nothing. You would, of course, have to be faithful to me. There could be no other."

Beryl was aghast. Such utter disregard for propriety. He dared to insult her by voicing such a corrupt and immoral arrangement. For his financial support, she was to become his mistress. He must think her desperate to suggest such a thing. Beryl was so shocked that she was at a loss for words.

He gave a nasty chuckle. "Your expression is one of affront, but I will tell you this arrangement is much more common than you think. Quite a lot of gentlemen have mistresses. Most, I would say."

Beryl gasped. "This conversation is entirely inappropriate, my lord. Surely, I did not give you cause to think that I would be open to such an arrangement."

"I will not apologize because it was your beauty that beguiled me. I am confident that I can speak for other gentlemen here. You will unlikely receive a marriage proposal, but I guarantee you will receive other proposals like mine," Lord Stanmore announced with a flourish.

Beryl wished that she could kick him in the shin.

How dare he! Was she destined only to meet rakes? "This may be socially accepted or ignored, but it will never be the life I choose. I have done nothing to warrant this unwanted attention. Lord Stanmore, let me be clear, it is unwanted."

To Lord Stanmore, her feelings seem irrelevant. He would have his mistress to enjoy and his wife to bear his legitimate children. How disgusting.

Lord Stanmore scoffed. "Lady Beryl, when I marry, it is to form an alliance. I know what my family will expect. I could—"

"I think you have said quite enough, Lord Stanmore. I am not interested." His lips flattened at her interruption, but he said no more. Beryl was relieved when the set came to an end.

He bowed to her and flashed a mocking smile she wished she could wipe from his face. He led her to the corner of the dance floor and left her there. Beryl said nothing further, and she was pleased Grace and Lady Ellsworth were still occupied. She needed a moment to compose herself. At first, she was optimistic about the season and the prospect of finding a husband, but now she was filled with trepidation and self-doubt. She did not want to believe what Lord Stanmore said was true, but what would she do if he was right?

CHAPTER 8

The ballroom was hot and stuffy. Beryl's fan made no difference to the stifling heat. She lowered it with a groan. Lady Ellsworth and Grace approached Beryl a few minutes later.

"Let us take a walk in the garden," Lady Ellsworth said.

A simple request but it was said with malice. Lady Ellsworth could not hide her look of disapproval.

"Yes. It will be much cooler there," Grace replied.

Her cousins led the way onto the terrace and into the garden. Beryl lifted her face to the sky and inhaled the cool night air. It was so fresh that she almost wished she could remain there rather than return to the maddening crush. They walked down the path surrounded by geraniums, petunias, and lilies. The sweet smell of violets reached her nostrils, although she did not see them. They arrived at a secluded place in the garden, and her cousins rounded on her.

"You were brought here to be Grace's chaperone, but I see you do not intend to perform your duties. After all that we have done for you. You are batting your eyes at every eligible bachelor here and taking away all the attention from Grace, and it is her season." Lady Ellsworth sneered, and her voice dripped with contempt.

Beryl was shocked to be accused of such a thing. "Lady Ellsworth, you are mistaken. I did not—"

Lady Ellsworth held up her hand to silence Beryl. "You will be quiet. We are not interested in your excuses."

Grace snorted loudly. So unladylike. Her hand was folded across her chest, and she drummed her fingers on her arm.

Beryl wondered if it would be best for her to keep quiet and not engage. She pressed her lips together to keep herself from speaking.

Lady Ellsworth's head shook from side to side in

disapproval. "You have commandeered the attention of Viscount Bowden and the Earl of Stanmore. You danced with *both* lords."

"I merely—" Beryl began before she was cut off.

Grace's eyes were cold. "Why would they choose to dance with you? Unless you beguiled them. You are spiteful and deceitful."

Beryl felt a tightening in her chest as she bore the brunt of their insults.

"Grace is right, and I am not of a mind to forget your transgression. You cannot be trusted. I want you to return to Chalfont House immediately and pack your things. You are not to be there when we return," Lady Ellsworth pronounced.

Beryl gasped, pressing her palm over her pounding heart. "Lady Ellsworth, there has been a terrible misunderstanding! I did not invite their attention, and it would have been scandalous to refuse!"

Beryl's gaze shifted to Grace, who flashed a triumphant smile.

A vein visibly throbbed in Lady Ellsworth's forehead. "You have taken us for fools. The misunderstanding was taking you into our home.

You do not deserve our generosity," Lady Ellsworth said before she spun around and walked toward the house, with Grace following closely behind.

Beryl stood frozen. All she wanted was the chance to find a husband so she would never have to suffer such indignities again, but she failed at even this task. Instead of her situation being better since she came to London, it was actually far worse.

It was more the pity that the eligible gentlemen who showed her attention thus far only were only interested in a mistress. None wanted a wife. The tears burned just as much as her humiliation. Was she to be condemned to society's scrap heap to live the life of a spinster? Fear rushed through her and Beryl trembled. She dreaded such an unfulfilling life.

If only her father had the foresight to …

Beryl gasped for air. She loved her father, but this was almost too much to bear. The lack of a dowry had placed her in a vulnerable position, and every time she thought things could not possibly get worse, they did. Sobs wracked Beryl and her shoulders shook. She was alarmed by how loud her sobs were. She balled her fist and bit down on it, but it did nothing to numb her pain. She was hurt, angry and disappointed. How could they treat her this way when she had done nothing wrong? Tears streamed down her face, and her heart ached.

She could not remain in London for the season, so there would be no prospect of finding a husband. Beryl's heart was racing, and she felt hot and flushed. Beryl felt the same fear that she felt when she was asked to leave her childhood home. She did not like the uncertainty, but she had been cast into a sea of it, and she had to think of a way to get out of it.

Her survival depended on it.

***

THEODORE HAD SEEN Lady Beryl and her cousins go into the garden, but only her cousins returned. He waited for a moment longer before he decided to check on her. He would be discreet. Theodore used an alternative entrance to the garden and searched for Lady Beryl. He heard the gentle whispers of her sobs before he saw her. He wondered at the cause of her distress, but he did not want to startle her. He stopped at a respectable distance.

"Lady Beryl. I do not mean to impose, but you

appear quite upset. What is causing you such distress?" Theodore ensured his tone was soothing.

Lady Beryl spun around to face him, and he could see her tear-streaked face. The tears did not detract from her beauty. She was stunning in the pale moonlight, and his heart drummed against his ribs. Theodore saw the pain in her eyes. He knew that it was really none of his affair, but he did not like that she was so upset.

"You always have a way of showing up uninvited," Lady Beryl snapped.

Her reaction caused Theodore to raise his brow, but she spoke before he could utter a word.

"I apologize, Lord Bowden. That was uncalled for." She sighed heavily.

Lady Beryl used her fingers to brush the tears away, and then she hiccupped.

Theodore gave her an understanding nod. "I will only accept your apology if you share what unsettled you."

He saw the emotions play out on her face, and it appeared that she was wrestling with deciding whether she would share the information or not. Yet, worry had creased her brows.

"You may find some relief if you unburden yourself of your troubles," Theodore gently urged.

Lady Beryl hesitated, then a breath shuddered from her. "There has been a terrible misunderstanding, and my cousins have said I need to return to Chalfont House immediately and pack my things."

Theodore lightly touched her shoulder. "What misunderstanding?"

Lady Beryl opened her mouth and then closed it. Theodore waited.

"You asked me to dance, and so did Earl Stanmore. My cousins concluded that I must be trying to win your favor and upstage cousin Grace."

Lady Beryl appeared drained and weighed down by the events, and his heart reached out to her. The poor woman. Had she not been through enough?

"What utter nonsense! I am sure your cousin would have received several requests to dance before the evening ended." Theodore wondered how her family could treat her this way.

Lady Beryl hiccupped. "You do not understand. They would only have been happy if I did not receive any attention at all. Now I must leave their home and make a way for myself. I cannot imagine what to do!"

Theodore lifted his hand and then lowered it.

"That would have been impossible. You are certainly the most beautiful woman in the room. I can assure you that every gentleman has noticed you."

Lady Beryl gave him a weak smile; at least the tears had stopped. He did not seek to flatter her. He could never tire of gazing at her comely features. Theodore felt the overwhelming need to fix the situation. There was a way that he could offer her support, and a thought formed in Theodore's mind. It could be the perfect solution for Lady Beryl's predicament and his.

Theodore flashed an encouraging smile. "I have a proposal that would be of mutual benefit."

Lady Beryl frowned before she cautiously asked, "A proposal?"

He tilted his head back. "Fear not. It is not the indecent sort. You may remember that I mentioned my nieces … Louise is seven and Mattie is five. They need a governess, and you are in need of a home. I am sure we can come to an arrangement."

"A governess!"

"Yes. Will you consider it?"

Lady Beryl rubbed the back of her neck. She shifted her weight from one leg to the next as if she could not get comfortable. She darted a gaze at his face. "After everything that has transpired between us, my lord, I am not sure that is a good idea."

Theodore hesitated and weighed his words. "All that transpired. Do you mean the kiss?" he casually asked.

Theodore's eyes dropped to her lips as he recalled their sweet taste and how she melted into the kiss. So responsive. He pushed the thought from his mind.

"Yes, the kiss," she said, flushing.

"I am not totally without honor, Lady Beryl. I do not have relations with women that are in my employ. It would be entirely inappropriate to carry on with a member of my household staff. If that is your concern, you need not worry."

The tension visibly left her. He continued, "If I am honest, I have not been the best of uncles. I have been absent for far too long, which has done nothing to help me connect with my nieces. I ... I do not know how ... how to be the father figure they need."

Lady Beryl's gaze flashed up to meet his, and the compassion pulled him into their depths. His heart squeezed. At this moment, he felt ashamed of his behavior toward the children. He did not deserve Lady Beryl's compassion.

"In what way do you deem yourself lacking?"

Theodore raked his fingers through his hair. This is not something he would want to discuss, but she deserved his honesty. "I am afraid I have not spent enough time talking and listening to them since William passed away. I may not agree with my uncle on many things, but on this, we agree. My nieces deserve more, and I should start looking out for their interests. You would make a good governess. You are a lady and clearly well educated."

Lady Beryl took a deep breath and smoothed her hands down her gown. "To be fair, I had thought of becoming a governess, but it meant accepting that I had fallen on hard times and needed to work to care for myself. Although it was an unfortunate situation I found myself in, I resisted the idea." Lady Beryl folded her hands across her chest and hugged herself.

"We did not discuss your wages. You will be paid three hundred pounds per year."

Beryl gasped. "That is very generous of you, my lord. I would be able to put money aside for my retirement."

Theodore waited and listened. Patience.

"Thank you for your kind offer. I will accept the position," she said.

Theodore rubbed his hands together. "Excellent, I will make arrangements with staff at Bowden Park. They will have a room prepared for you. I will not tarry in London. I have matters of business to attend to, but once that is done, I will return to the countryside. You should go to Chalfont House, pack your belongings, and take them to Bowden Park. I will arrange a carriage to collect you as the stage can be uncomfortable."

This time, her smile was heartfelt, and it radiated with loveliness. His gaze was fixed on her soft lips. Their kiss played across Theodore's mind even though he tried not to think about it. A pleasant chill ran over his skin and tingled down his spine. He wanted to take her into his arms right now. It was possible; after all, they were somewhere private. Theodore heard her gasp, and when his gaze found her eyes, he saw a soft flame flicker in their depths. He was warmed by the knowledge that she felt it too.

The air was charged between them, and there did not seem to be enough. His breath caught in his throat. The impulse to taste her lips was almost overpowering. Theodore's heart was already at a quick trot that raced toward a gallop. Theodore could not resist.

"There is something that I need right now." He was almost taken aback by the edgy rasp in his voice.

She held his gaze, and it was dark and intense. His heart thumped, one beat, then another as he remained lost in her captive blue eyes. Her tongue quickly darted out and licked her lips. His mouth went dry. He needed to take those lips between his teeth. Why was this happening when he vowed to control himself?

"What do you need?" Her voice was a whisper.

Theodore was attuned to her as she took a step forward. She was not hesitant.

"A final kiss. Now that you have accepted the position, we will maintain propriety. This will be the last time. I desperately want to … need to kiss you."

Her cheeks flushed and she stepped forward and leaned into him. "Kiss me. I want it."

Her soft rosy scent filled his nostrils. His desire caused him to swallow hard. Theodore tilted her chin and his mouth covered hers. He groaned his longing when she opened to him, and he tasted her wet heat. She made a soft sigh of pleasure, and he pulled her to him. Their tongues searched and probed, lighting a fire of need that he struggled to control. Fierce desire washed over him, and he felt the tightening in his breeches. He must stop. He wanted to, but just as he was about to pull away, a soft whimper escaped her, and it hung in the air between them. Theodore deepened the kiss, pulling her closer so that he could mold her body against his hard form.

Her mouth was hot and ready, and she followed his lead when he moved to nibble at her lips. She tasted so damn good. He captured her tongue and sucked on it, and he felt his cock strain against the fabric. He was sure she knew how much he wanted her. Surely, she must feel it. He wanted to feel her warmth around his … This time, he stopped.

Theodore heard his labored breathing and to think it was only a bloody kiss. Had he ever felt hunger this visceral? Lady Beryl took a step back, but not before he saw the smoldering heat in her eyes.

"As I said, I will accept the position, but we need to establish the ground rules."

He could hear the slight tremor in her voice, and he was pleased to know that he affected her so.

Theodore chuckled. "Rules? What could those possibly be, Lady Beryl? Enlighten me." His own voice was husky and sounded deeper than it normally would be.

She touched her lips, and the simple action made him struggle to control himself. He wanted to take her mouth once more, to demand, explore, and cajole.

Lady Beryl gave him a stern stare that pinned him where he stood. "There will be no more kissing," she said decisively, a spot of color had risen on her cheeks. "That was our final embrace."

A flicker of excitement settled in the depths of his belly, only dampened by the thought of the promise that he was about to make. *Bloody hell*! After the way they just kissed, it would be damned near impossible, but he must try. He gave her his word. Only moments ago, he told her she would not be taken advantage of.

He nodded in acquiescence. "Agreed."

She continued, "You will decide what I may teach your nieces, but I will decide how to teach them. You are not to interfere with my methods of teaching, my lord."

Theodore thought about it for a moment and wondered if this would return to haunt him. He could not immediately think of a reason to refuse. "Agreed."

"Finally, I must have Sundays off."

That was fair enough. He did not expect her to work every day.

"Agreed." All he could think about was the fact that he agreed there would be no kissing because he quite enjoyed it. This was not going to be easy. He sighed. How the hell was he going to stick with it?

CHAPTER 9

Bowden Park, Buckinghamshire

Inexplicably, Beryl had allowed Lord Bowden to kiss her. In hindsight it was utterly reckless and ruinous, but also wonderful. The very memory of the kiss caused her heart to beat erratically, and a crackling liveliness surged through her veins. She may like the touch of his lips and his taste, but this would be the last time. She meant it. *No more kissing.*

She was already in a vulnerable position, and she could not afford to be careless. As a governess, Beryl must be gentle, modest, reserved, and dignified. Modesty and dignified reserve did not provide enough of a deterrent to some unscrupulous gentlemen who were determined to take liberties with an unprotected lady. She was grateful that Theodore offered her protection, but she would not fall into his bed and become his lover. Even if his kisses were delightful, and he revealed himself to not only be a charming rogue, but also a gentleman who was considerate.

Beryl used the next week to pack her belongings, and they had agreed she would send word to Lord Bowden when she was ready to depart. He sent a grand carriage and footmen to escort her to Bowden Park, and Beryl was pleased to see he was treating her with this kind consideration. Beryl did not travel far since Chalfont House and Bowden Park were neighboring estates. When Beryl arrived at the viscount's estate, she was surprised to find Lord Bowden there to greet her.

A footman helped her down, and she dipped into a curtsy. "My lord," she greeted.

"Welcome to Bowden Park, Lady Beryl. You have arrived at an opportune moment because I was just about to run an errand on the estate. Would you like to accompany us? My steward, Mr. Fogg, will also be riding along," Lord Bowden said.

She was curious to see more of his home. "Thank you, my lord. I will."

"Good. I will have them arrange the horses, and you can meet me in the courtyard when you have changed."

He spun around and disappeared with purposeful strides. The butler led Beryl upstairs in the direction of her trunks. She quickly found her riding habit and dressed. She descended the stairs and met Lord Bowden and his steward in the courtyard. Lord Bowden had made the introductions before he took them on a tour of the estate grounds. It was a pleasant day; although it was cloudy, it did not rain.

The viscount was riding slightly ahead of her, and Mr. Fogg was behind. Lord Bowden hung back as the trail widened. "I remembered you liked riding just as much as I."

Beryl glanced at him. "Yes. It is so relaxing; how could I not?"

"When I am in London, it is what I miss most. Riding is not quite the same there."

"I agree. I went riding whenever I got the chance, which was almost every day at Penrose Hall," Beryl said, smiling.

"You ride well. Gracefully."

"Thank you, my lord." She felt the heat rise on her cheeks. Beryl did not know why she was flushing at such a simple compliment. "When we first met, I could tell you liked horses. He is a beautiful beast."

Lord Bowden chuckled and patted his horse. "That he is."

"If you do not mind me asking, have you told the children they will have a new governess?"

"I have, indeed."

Beryl flashed him a smile, but she was a bit nervous about meeting them. This would be her first position as a governess, and she wanted to get it right. What if the children did not like her?

Good heavens.

What if they were absolute terrors? She had her doubts, but she certainly would not mention them to the viscount. Beryl had never particularly liked the idea of being a governess because her position was lowered, but she accepted that she had no choice. It was a new life, so it held some excitement, the unknown. Yet, she knew that she must do whatever she could so that she could gain valuable experience that she would need when she moved to another family. She would also need good references. She hoped she would be treated with respect and dignity.

What she had seen of the house and grounds so

far was divine. She would enjoy exploring, so it was important for her to know she could have some time for herself.

"They are very excited to meet you."

"As I am looking forward to meeting them," Beryl said, glancing at his side profile. How austere he seemed. "You appear contemplative, my lord."

A small frown creased his forehead. "Riding across the estate reminds me so much of William. He was the one who oversaw the everyday maintenance of the estate, the farm, which provides a great deal of food for the house, and any legal disputes. I would sometimes tag along," Lord Bowden said. "To be fair, I did not pay as much attention. It was William who would inherit the title and lands. Why did I need to bother? I need to make up for that now."

"It is fortunate that he had you, and you shared such a bond."

A wry smile touched his mouth. "I suppose so, although if you listen to my uncle, I am making a muck of it."

"Do not be too hard on yourself, my lord. We all deal with our grief in different ways. It takes some of us much longer than others to adjust to life without the ones we love."

They both turned to face each other, and their gazes locked before Beryl quickly looked away. Her heart fluttered at his penetrating gaze.

"Wise words," he said.

They rode in silence for a moment before he spoke.

"My uncle believes that I have been shirking my responsibility. I should be present and not gallivanting around Europe," Theodore said.

Beryl chuckled. "I do not suppose you took that well."

Theodore smiled and her heart quickened. The man was far too charming.

"No. I was never one to obey rules. Society has quite a few rules that I think are nonsensical. I am sure that, on the whole, people can make sound decisions for themselves without any interference," he said.

"I was not as lucky as you. My governess was quite strict, and it worked to keep me controlled as a child. There were so many rules that I am surprised I remember them all," Beryl said with a light laugh. "It must be fun to break the rules at times." *Like I did when I attended that masquerade ball.* A part of her wished for more experiences like that even as Beryl's practical heart warned her to always be circumspect.

"That must have been terribly boring," he murmured, his stare far too assessing.

It felt as if he stripped her bare. Swallowing, Beryl said, "I hardly think so, my lord. It was the norm. It was accepted."

"I see," Theodore said.

"Though I confess at times the rules were sometimes confusing. For one, I was expected to keep abreast of the news and to be well informed, but in the same breath, I was not expected to voice my opinion. Quite contradictory."

"I suppose you were required to know enough to participate in a conversation but not enough to overshadow it. A fine art."

"Hmm. Why should I be concerned about overshadowing the conversation? If I took the time to be well informed, should the gentlemen not do the same? In that case, we could have a lively debate rather than me agreeing with everything he says. Surely, that would be more interesting. Would you not agree?" Beryl asked him pointedly.

Theodore grinned. "I take your point, but I do not see the *haut ton* agreeing with you. They would dispense with their own brand of justice for non-conformity."

"I know this to be true, but I shall never understand the logic of it."

"I often feel the same way."

She arched a brow. "I hardly think our situations, a lady and a gentleman, are comparable, Lord Bowden."

Theodore reined in his horse. "Whatever do you mean?"

"If we were to remain on the topic of conversation, you could easily insert a double-entendre, and it would be considered amusing. According to Miss Marsh, my governess, it would be detestable if I were to do the same, and no man would show me respect. Worst yet, if it were done in a gentleman's presence, he would be disgusted, and no one would have a good opinion of me."

Good humor danced in his eyes. "An interesting argument, although I must say if I used a double-entendre, I would expect any polite lady to pretend she did not hear it."

She smiled. "You are quite right. We could not laugh even if it were amusing."

"Hmm. I see. Why don't you come and play with me?" he drawled, deviltry dancing in his eyes.

Beryl tensed, and a shiver ran down her spine. It was as if he reached out and touched her from the back of her neck down to her spine. The viscount wore a wicked grin, and she felt a sense of relief. He was only teasing her. *The rogue*! With a sense of astonishment, Beryl realized she found the excursion quite pleasant, and she was pleasantly surprised by his teasing.

"In addition to your wages, I will also arrange for you to have a governess dress of sorts so you will be appropriately attired when you carry out your duties."

"Thank you, my lord."

"Do you not think that we can dispense with the formalities when we are alone? You can call me Theodore."

"If you insist, Theodore. However, I will still be Lady Beryl."

There was something electric between them, and she felt drawn to him, somehow, despite all her reasons to stay away. She had felt it by the lake when they first kissed, and it was even stronger than the last time. If they were to maintain an entirely professional relationship, it would not do to become too familiar.

Theodore chuckled. "As you wish, Lady Beryl."

They had just arrived at the village. Theodore and the steward went off to meet with the farmers. Apparently, the viscount had established a farmers' cooperative of some sort. The farmers were coming together to discuss advancements in how they grew crops and modern machinery. Theodore was informing them of things he had learned on the continent. It seems that he was not only cavorting, but he had actually learned a thing or two that he thought he could adopt at Bowden Park.

Interestingly, he tried to portray himself as such a bounder who thrived on a carefree existence, but clearly, there was more to him than that. Evidently, he had chosen not to worry about the position he found himself cast in, and he worried even less about the *haut ton*. In all their encounters thus far, he seemed relaxed and carefree, while Beryl tended to worry. It was only when her father became ill that she became a worrier, for she, too, had a more carefree existence. She had no need to be concerned about her welfare because she had always been provided for.

Now everything is so different, she silently said, suppressing her sigh.

They had gone off to the meeting hall, and Beryl decided she wanted to remain outdoors. She dismounted and started to stretch her legs, smiling when the horse followed. It was a fine animal. The viscount had great taste in horses.

Beryl's thoughts turned to the viscount's nieces. She was sure she was perfectly capable of teaching a seven-year-old and a five-year-old. She could hardly say that the role would suit her perfectly because it was not what she wished for herself. She had never envisioned what it would be like living in someone's household and taking care of their children. Would she be any good at working for someone? Beryl closed her eyes and swiftly prayed. She truly hoped it would not be awful and that she would not come to regret it.

CHAPTER 10

They had just returned to Bowden Park, and the steward bid his farewell. They could hear the girls' shrieks, and it appeared to be coming from the garden.

"This seems to be a good time for you to meet the children," Theodore said.

"Very well," Beryl replied with a small smile.

They proceeded down the path in the direction of shrieks and giggles until they came upon the girls. They chased each other around the fountain, engrossed in their romping.

"Louise and Mattie, come here please. Your governess is here," Theodore said.

Both girls spun around to face them, and they

immediately stopped giggling. They walked hand in hand toward Theodore.

"Girls, this is Lady Beryl. May I present Louise and Mattie?"

Both girls curtsied and said, "I am pleased to meet you, Lady Beryl."

"I remember mother said that one day we would have a governess," Louise said, her gaze wide and curious.

"Mother is in heaven with the angels, Lady Beryl. That is what uncle said and I cannot visit her," Mattie said as her lashes grew wet with tears.

Beryl could not imagine the pain these children felt. The poor darlings had lost both their mother and father and the pain was unimaginable. She knew that it was impossible to protect a child from the pain of a loss, and it would be an ongoing process. She could only try to make Louise and Mattie feel safe. Louise was not as emotional as Mattie, which was understandable since she was the eldest. Surely, they would cope with their grief differently. As Beryl knew all too well, there was no right or wrong way to grieve. She was an emotional wreck when her father passed away, and she was overwhelmed by the pain. Healing was a journey. Kindness and patience were what the girls needed.

Beryl dropped to her knees and gazed at each girl in turn. "I am very pleased to meet you both. I know you are feeling very sad because you lost your mother. I am feeling sad too. You see, I lost my father. You loved your mother very much, and I loved my father, and I would like you to remember that your mother loved you very much."

Louise smiled, showing her missing tooth. "Yes, Lady Beryl. She always told us."

Mattie's voice trembled as she said, "I have been sad ever since mother died. I miss her, and when I think of her, sometimes it makes me cry."

Theodore inhaled sharply, and Beryl suspected this was the first he heard of Mattie's sorrow.

Beryl reached her hand to brush away a tear that made its way down Mattie's cheek. "It is permissible to cry, Mattie. Crying can make you feel less sad because it goes away for a little while. I cried for my father."

Both girls' eyebrows shot up.

"You did?" Louise asked.

"Yes," Beryl replied.

"And it made you feel better?"

"It did indeed." Beryl placed a hand on her heart. "I found releasing the feelings I had inside, rather than keeping them here, was very helpful."

"Oh," Mattie said in wonderment.

"I am sad, but sometimes I am angry. Both mother and father are gone. We have no parents," Louise said.

"It is normal to feel angry too, and eventually, the anger will also get less," Beryl said.

She could only imagine the girls' heartbreak, angst, uncertainty, and anxiety.

"Mother was pretty, like you, Lady Beryl," Mattie said, breaking the somber moment.

They all laughed and Beryl stood. She turned to face Theodore, and his gaze bored into her. It made her feel naked, and Beryl's heart began to flutter.

"Shall we return to the house? It is almost time for dinner," Theodore said.

Mattie immediately perked up. "Let us race to the house, Louise."

Off Mattie went in a mad dash down the path before Louise shouted after her.

"That is not fair, Mattie. I did not count to three." Louise complained before she rushed after her sister, her curls bobbing from side to side.

Beryl laughed.

"Lady Beryl, would you join us for dinner?" Theodore asked.

Beryl gave a start. She was not expecting it. Her

governess did not usually eat with her unless her parents invited her to join them or to attend a dinner party. She wondered if governesses of genteel birth found such an invitation pleasant and refreshing or if it reminded them of their past status in society. It could be awkward and difficult, or perhaps they hated it.

Theodore was offering her a way to live in the way that she was accustomed to. He was being quite charitable, and she appreciated his kindness.

"Thank you, Theodore. I shall," Beryl replied.

As they walked toward the house, Theodore said, "You were very good with the children. I must admit I have been a bit selfish. I thought more about my own grief and the new demands and less about what they have been experiencing. The way you spoke of grief made me realize how foolish I have been."

Beryl stopped, and they both turned to face each other.

"I meant what I said, Theodore. We all grieve in different ways. Who am I to say the way you are grieving is wrong? It is enough that you recognize that the girls need you."

"I think you would get on very well with my uncle. He is sure to visit as soon as he discovers you are here. I am beginning to think he has a spy in my household."

"Considering how we met, are you certain you want to accuse someone of spying?"

Theodore threw back his head and gave a hearty laugh, which caused his shoulders to shake. "Touché."

"I suppose you do not normally eat with the children."

"I do not. I certainly do not intend to eat with them every day, but I wanted to do it tonight."

"It is not for me to say how you should treat your nieces," Beryl said.

"One thing that I can say about you, Lady Beryl, is that you are refreshingly direct. This stood out from the first day that we met. Please feel free to speak frankly," Theodore encouraged.

"Well, the girls need support to manage their emotions and to feel secure. They want to feel that they are loved and understood."

"I believe you are right, but I must admit that I feel ill-equipped to do these things. I am actually quite relieved that you are here to assist me," Theodore said.

Later that evening, in the sanctuary of her room, Beryl recalled the conversation. Theodore's words had warmed her. He should not be having this effect on her. She reminded herself that her feelings would only cause her trouble. She must not be tempted to give in to them and risk her position. She was penniless. Her honor and virtue were all that she had, and they were priceless. To risk losing them would be foolhardy. It is a harsh fate, but she already had a sample of the world's cruelty.

She had only just arrived and being a governess was not so bad … so far so good. It would all be fine as long as she remained ladylike, modest, and respectable. If she lost her head with the viscount, it would not go well for her.

I must be clever and maintain my composure.

Theodore wanted to be the veritable bachelor, daunted by marriage, and she needed a husband. If it was one thing that she knew, water and oil do not mix. She deserved more and better than he was prepared to give. Beryl would ensure that the dresses Theodore commissioned for her would be modest and that she was dressed neatly and becomingly. She would do whatever she could to retain this position and gain experience which would serve her well later when she moved on. It was inevitable that she would leave once the girls were grown.

Beryl was fortunate because a governess did not always have her own room. She had a small, private sitting room as well. She had written to Flora, and she was pleased to receive a reply, but she had not had a chance to read it. Sitting on the window ledge, she opened the letter.

Dearest Beryl,

I was pleased to receive your letter and to know you are well. I was worried when you left London in such a hurry, yet I know you would not have done so without good reason. Your cousins have acted in a way that showed their true character, or should I say lack thereof. Shame on them. I regret that you found yourself in such a dire situation. I know it would not have been an easy decision to make, to become a governess knowing it will ruin your chances of finding a husband and having children. You have resigned yourself to a life of solitude.

It saddens me to know that because of their selfishness your status has been highly impacted. However, given that no one in society has caught wind of this, it may not be so detrimental yet. Let us explore the available options. My dear, you are now unchaperoned in the home of one of London's most eligible bachelors, and this may very well be in your favor. This is especially advantageous given he has kissed you twice. Your letter said you enjoyed being kissed and you are pleased to be in the lord's company. I think you will be well served by trying to make him fall in love with you, therefore securing marriage, in which case you would not give up the things you desire most.

If that does not work, then at least you should get a taste of passion before you fully commit to your life of loneliness. Do write to me to let me know how you get on and I anxiously await your news.

Sincerely,

Flora

Shocked and with her heart pounding a fierce tempo, Beryl read Flora's letter for a second time. She had two options. Make Theodore fall in love with her or give in to illicit passion. Beryl pressed a palm over her chest and leaned her forehead on the cool glass.

Is this why I am unable to push him from my dreams? Because I want him so?

The heat racing along her skin provided the answer. She worried at her bottom lip with her teeth for a few moments. Beryl wanted the viscount to fall in love with her.

Oh, is it truly possible or am I leading my heart to ruin and heartbreak?

CHAPTER 11

Theodore was sitting in the library attending to some of the myriad of correspondence that awaited his attention. He was not fond of going through them, but there was no point in procrastinating any further. He sat around his large oak desk, staring at the to-do pile, which was slowly whittling down. Several minutes later he found that he was thinking about Lady Beryl when replying to practically every letter.

You are being ridiculous! he chastised himself. *Why is it so hard to not think about her?*

Lady Beryl was interesting if she was not anything else. She had laid down the rules for him after they had shared not one, but two passionate kisses. He was amused by the surety in her tone when she insisted she would remain Lady Beryl. Theodore chuckled. Her beauty was not easy to overlook, but there was much more to her. She was spirited, yet she had a kind temperament, and she was prepared to take the high ground to find some peace in life. The combination made her sweetly alluring, and it was admirable because life had not always been kind to her. She was rare and he was captivated.

She was a gentle soul, yet what had he done? When they met for the second time, he kissed her without permission and told her he wanted a mistress and not a wife. Then in the garden he kissed her again, and it was such a sweet kiss. She wanted him, and that thought made his cock stir. *Damn it.*

He would not act on it. As her employer, it would not be right to kiss and seduce her. It was just as well that she set the rules. It was the right thing to do to protect herself, and it is a reminder that he must be responsible. For him to act on his lust would be a potential disaster. Lady Beryl being at Bowden Park was not for him, but rather for Louise and Mattie. He would stop thinking about her and focus on what he needed to do to ensure the estate was well run and allow her to care for the children.

THE VISCOUNT'S DARING CINDERELLA

It had been a bit over a week since Lady Beryl arrived, and Theodore thought she was a godsend. The children seemed to have settled into a pleasant routine. In addition to teaching the children, she adopted a motherly behavior and became a protector and caregiver for the children. She was working wonders with them already.

Theodore pushed his chair back and decided to go for a stroll. He would see what Lady Beryl and the children were doing. He went to the tutor room, but it was empty. What was the meaning of this? Theodore expected the children to be in their lessons. He moved to the window and looked outside to find Lady Beryl and the children playing with a ball.

He bounded down the stairs, through the main door and down to the far corner of the lawn. Lady Beryl and the children were in a circle, and they were passing a ball between them. As he grew closer, he could hear them singing.

One potato, two potato, three potato, four.
Five potato, six potato, seven potato, more!

They were so engrossed in the game that they did not see him approach. They began to pass the ball and sing the song a bit faster. He looked at the ball and realized it was the same rubber ball he and William used to play with, although they played football. His heart squeezed at the fond memory.

Maddie dropped the ball. "Oops. I suppose that potato was too hot."

They all began giggling.

Louise looked up and beckoned to Theodore. "Will you join us, Uncle?"

Theodore could think of a number of things that required his attention, but he saw the plea in the children's eyes. He could certainly spare a few moments.

Lady Beryl's eyes twinkled. "Yes, please join us."

Theodore nodded. "Very well."

"Louise, what can you tell your uncle about the game."

"Uncle, we must pretend to have a steaming hot potato in our hands and pass it around. Make sure to let go of it as quickly as possible so you will not get burnt." Louise said.

"Ah, I see," Theodore replied.

"And Mattie, can you tell your uncle the song's words?"

"Yes, Lady Beryl. One potato, two potato, three

potato, four. Five potato, six potato, seven potato, more!" Mattie sang.

"Well done, girls. Shall we get started?"

They began passing the ball to each other and singing the song, and with each round, they passed the ball and sang faster. Lady Beryl passed the ball much faster than he anticipated, and it fell to the ground before he could catch it.

The children began to giggle as they could not contain their amusement.

"That was rather clumsy, Uncle," Louise said with an impish grin.

Theodore laughed. "I am afraid I am not as good as you at this game. You need to teach me."

"Truly?" Mattie asked.

"Yes," Theodore replied.

The girls glanced at each other, delighted, and his heart once again squeezed.

"Let us start again," Lady Beryl said.

At first, Theodore thought the game was a bit silly, but he actually enjoyed it. He liked that the girls no longer seemed so morose. He took great pleasure in hearing Lady Beryl's laughter, like the tinkling of a bell. Her face flushed and returned to its usual stoic expression when she caught him staring at her.

When he dropped the ball the second time, Mattie exclaimed, "Oh dear! I think you need to have some lessons with our governess, Uncle."

Lady Beryl had a hearty laugh at his expense. Her laughter was so intense that tears pooled in her eyes, and she gasped for breath between each bout of mirth. She was so lovely when she appeared carefree. As if she had no need to worry about how she might seem to the outside world. Her eyes crinkled, and when her lips parted, it showed her beautiful white teeth.

I am bloody smitten, he groused silently; *even her teeth I think beautiful*. Theodore raked his fingers through his hair, a sense of bemusement creeping over his senses.

Lady Beryl wiped her eyes, her cheeks flushed with the exertion, a satisfied sigh escaping her lips.

It was the sigh that made him forget himself. What it would be like to hear her sigh of pleasure once more. He remembered all too well when she sighed against his lips, her hot breath scorching him with desire. His cock jumped, and he willed himself to behave. This was neither the time nor the place.

"Girls, it is time for lunch. Go ahead and wash up. I shall join you shortly."

The girls ran toward the house, and he was finally alone with Lady Beryl.

She raised a brow. "Was there something you wanted to speak with me about, my lord?"

"Not particularly. I searched for you in the tutor room, and you were not there."

"I see," Lady Beryl replied.

"That is where I expected you to be," Theodore said.

"You do remember we had established the rules, do you not, Theodore?"

"I do, but you can hardly call this teaching," he said.

Beryl scoffed. "That is where you are wrong."

"Is that so?"

She could not mask her annoyance. "Most assuredly. Children do not only learn in the tutor room, my lord. In our game, the children improved their speed, agility, ball skills, hand-eye coordination, and attention span."

Theodore inclined his head to the side and continued to scrutinize her. "I take your point. I did not look at it quite that way."

Her eyes flashed. "Preciscly. I will just remind you that the rule is I will decide how to teach."

"You are right, Lady Beryl. I will not interfere."

Theodore was struggling to keep a straight face. Her voice was so haughty and high-handed.

"I bid you good afternoon, my lord," she said as she left him standing on the lawn.

Theodore could not tear his eyes away from her swaying hips. He felt considerably discomposed when he pictured himself holding onto those hips in the heat of passion. The cock that he was trying to tame strained against his breeches. Apparently, Lady Beryl was obsessed with the rules. He remembered them. How could he forget? If there was to be no kissing, he had no idea why his thoughts drifted to further intimacy. An odd feeling throbbed in his mind, yet he could not decipher what it was. This infernal longing to be with her was becoming intolerable.

The fact that she enjoyed being kissed did not help, but he must be the one to steel himself. What he just observed with Beryl and the children served to solidify what he was thinking earlier today. He would be a fool not to acknowledge how well she has done with the children. Surely, he could not ruin that for them by seducing Beryl. That would be utterly selfish, particularly as Theodore knew from experience that liaisons could turn bad quickly, especially with inexperienced ladies. Often after a liaison, a lady would expect marriage, and he would not offer it. He knew they both needed to maintain their composure under the circumstances, but when she stirred his blood in the way that she did, how the hell was he going to manage?

CHAPTER 12

A few more days passed since Theodore played the hot potato game with the girls and Lady Beryl. Despite his resolve, his yearning to be with her, laughing and chatting, and certainly kissing and more, haunted his sleep. So what he did was try his best to avoid being alone with her. Theodore buried himself in work and had a later supper this evening alone. He wished it could have been with her and that he could have seen her smile or heard her tinkling laugh.

Theodore scowled, stood up from the sofa, and poured himself a glass of bourbon. He heard the library door open, and he spun around and came face-to-face with Lady Beryl.

A soft gasp escaped her. "I do apologize, my lord."

"I did not mean to startle you, forgive me." He was apologizing for being in his own library. Now, he was being really ridiculous.

A strained chuckle came from her. "I did not realize you were here. You are not usually here at this time, my lord."

Ah, so it seems the lady was also avoiding being alone with him.

She fidgeted a bit under his regard and said, "I came to get a book to read before retiring."

"Please come in."

"Only if I am not intruding," Lady Beryl said tentatively as she waited in the doorway.

There was an unfathomable watchfulness in her eyes that made his breath catch in his throat. He raked his gaze the full length of her. His first impulse was to send her away or leave the room because it had been such a struggle to keep her from his thoughts. He resisted the impulse and said, "I was having a nightcap, and you are not intruding. Will you join me?"

She came into the room. "A nightcap?"

He lifted the decanter. "Yes, bourbon. It is whiskey from America."

A smile touched her gorgeous lips and enigmatic eyes landed on his. "How exotic."

An odd sensation fluttered in his belly, and he struggled to dismiss it from his awareness. "Would you like to try it? I know you have a sense of adventure."

She canted her head. "I will try it. But how did you conclude that I have a sense of adventure?"

Theodore poured her a glass and handed it to her.

Lady Beryl took a small sip. "Err … This is not to my liking."

Theodore laughed. "I suppose it is an acquired taste."

They were both standing close to his desk, gazing at each other. Everything else in the room seemed to blur and fade except them.

Something indecipherable flashed in her eyes. "You were about to tell me about my sense of adventure," she murmured huskily.

"Are you certain you wish to know? It might shock you."

Humor gleamed in her gaze. "Then I invite you to shock me."

Did she realize her tone was like a sensual purr?

By God, Theodore felt as if he teetered on the edge of madness. "Just before the start of the season, you attended a ball that genteel ladies do not usually attend."

A soft gasp escaped her. He watched the emotions play over her features—alarm, doubt, and then caution, before her stoic expression returned. It was mere moments. How impressive. The lady would make an excellent gambler.

She lifted her chin. "What ball do you refer to?"

He had to hand it to her. She recovered quite well. He took a step closer to her and drawled, "The masquerade ball where you were dressed as an owl."

Her lips parted but no sound emerged. She stood transfixed.

"You were there?" Lady Beryl asked, pressing her palm over her chest.

He imagined that her heart was pounding. She seemed anxious that he mentioned it, and he was captivated. Her vulnerability, however fleeting, tugged at his senses. Somewhere in his mind it occurred to him that he was becoming too intrigued by her. It alarmed Theodore and he was unsure what to make of it. He tried so hard not to think of her because he wanted to honor the promise he made to himself.

"Yes, and we danced."

Her eyes widened and then she gasped, "You were the wizard!"

Theodore's heart stirred. "Indeed. Who was the pirate?"

"My dear friend Lady Flora Ely."

"Ahh. So, now you know what I meant. Only someone with an adventurous spirit would have dared attend that masquerade ball." Theodore teased her to lighten the mood because he could not deny the powerful attraction simmering in the air. He was never any good at tempering his desires, but *by God* he had made such an effort these past couple of weeks. Ever since she had come into his life, he felt an odd sort of imbalance.

Why, damn it? Why is she wreaking havoc on my senses?

The candle threw a glow over her face, and he wished she was not so enchantingly beautiful. Heat stirred in his loins. He had never wanted to take a lover to his bed as much as he wanted to take Beryl. Right here, right now. He should not do it. Theodore slammed his eyes closed. *I must not!*

"Yes," she said in a breathy whisper as if she

referred to something else. "I daresay I was a bit ... audacious that night."

He snapped his eyes open. Theodore's heart pounded in anticipation. "I believe you saw something wicked that greatly interested you that night."

Her eyes widened at the memory, and suddenly, the air was charged. He reached up and touched the tip of a finger to her lips, and she leaned into him.

"Do you know, I have never wanted another as I want you." Even to his ears, Theodore sounded harsh ... desperate.

Her stare appeared intrigued.

"I confess I like the notion that I can drive a man such as yourself mad with want."

Bloody hell. Her honesty would be the death of him. The lady was not flirting, merely speaking her truth.

She tucked a wisp of hair behind her ear. "I never imagined desire could be this dangerous."

A torrent of feelings raged in the pit of his stomach. "Go," he said hoarsely. She did not flee, merely stared at him with that enigmatic look in her eyes. Something said he should be wary, and he almost laughed at himself. He was the one society called a rake. He was the one with experience.

"Do you know what I want to do with you, Beryl?"

"Kiss me," she said softly. "I can see the need in your eyes."

"You are not running."

Her throat worked on a swallow. "I am not running. But I might slap your cheek …"

If you dare, remained unspoken.

Theodore took both glasses and placed them on the table. He pulled her tightly against him, and the floral notes of her perfume hung in the air. The room grew warmer, matching only his body heat, as he lightly stroked her cheeks then played his fingers across her lips once more. They parted for him, and he could feel her warm breath on his fingers. He desperately wanted to taste her mouth, but he would not. Theodore used the back of his fingers to trace her jawline down to her throat, and he could feel the rhythmic beat of her pulse. She sucked in a breath, flushing.

He took advantage of her low-cut dress, using a feather-light touch to caress her décolletage. Her bosom heaved as she strained for his touch. Her eyelids fluttered shut and when they reopened there was molten desire. Beryl's breath came in short gasps. The round swell of her breast tempted him, and he gave in. He reached into her dress and pried one nipple free. Her stiff nipple left no doubt that she was aroused, and he caressed it between his finger and thumb. She held on to his shoulders, and a soft sound escaped her. Theodore rolled and pinched the nipple as Beryl dug her nails into his shoulders and strained against him. Still, he did not kiss her.

He reached for the nipple and flicked his finger across the sensitive mound, kneading it. His cock was hard, and he pulled her close so she could rock against him. She could feel how much he wanted her. There was no denying the raw, wild need between them.

Theodore stood and reversed positions with Beryl. Her back was now toward his desk, and he lifted her so she sat on the desk. He raised her skirt and parted her legs with every inch of the urgency he felt. She was not wearing hose, and he ran his hands along her upper thighs uninhibited. He rested his forehead against hers, and he breathed in her moan of pleasure when his fingers played lightly over the apex of her thighs.

Theodore's heart was pounding in his chest. He

pulled his hand away, but Beryl moved forward, straining for him to return. She wanted him to touch her there. His hand reached for that most womanly part of her, and when he stroked her, it sent her into shivers of ecstasy. He slid a finger inside her, and she gasped and clenched around him. She was slippery wet. He stroked her deeply with one strong finger before he inserted two, igniting her. She writhed against his hand, lost in pleasure. At first, his strokes were deep and slow, but as she moaned and writhed, he increased the tempo. Moisture beaded between her legs. Her hard nub cried out to him, and he teased it as she arched her hips against his hand, demanding more of him.

"Theodore," she cried out as she found her release. She trembled in his arms.

He nuzzled her neck. "I am here," he whispered as she rode the waves of her pleasure.

They were both breathing hard as if they had made a mad dash. Theodore withdrew his fingers and helped Beryl to straighten her garments. Her face was flushed when she met his eyes; she lowered her lashes.

Theodore tilted her chin and gazed into her

eyes. Desire still burned hot, and it took all of his restraint not to take her right here.

"I submit my cheek for your slap."

He was rewarded with a smile. "You should not be ashamed or fear your passion, Beryl; it is natural and honest," he murmured. "I am sure you will agree that we are long past formalities."

"We are," she whispered.

"You found pleasure without breaking your rule. We did not kiss," Theodore said.

"But this is far more intimate than kissing. I should take kissing off the list and put whatever this is on it," Beryl gasped. "This is … *wicked*."

"Did you not enjoy it?" Theodore asked, although he already knew the answer.

Beryl stared at him with wide-eyed innocence. "Immensely. I might even want to experience it again."

Theodore chuckled, pulled her close, and gave her a tight hug. He sighed deeply.

"I want to as well, over and over, but I am afraid that I would not be able to control myself. I have not reached my pleasure, and it would be risky for me to do so. If I did, there is a chance you could be with child," he said, giving her the unvarnished truth. He is determined never to deceive this woman.

"Oh," she murmured.

She rested her head against his shoulder, and he wrapped his arms around her waist. *This feels … right.* An almost weak feeling assailed him at the awareness of how perfect she fitted against him.

Beryl squeezed him closer, and Theodore kissed the top of her head then withdrew from her embrace. It was time for them to separate before they went too far.

Beryl stared up at him. Her gaze was on his mouth, and he groaned at the desire in the depth of her eyes. "I want you to kiss me," Beryl said.

Theodore's breath caught in his throat.

"Do you not want to?"

The question was so simple, but a torrent of emotions went through him. He wanted to taste her more than anything. Theodore swiftly lowered his head and moved his mouth over hers with the desperate passion that he felt. He groaned at the first taste of her mouth, reveling in the taste of her lips. She softened instantly and opened her mouth to receive him. She gave a soft, irresistible moan, and he swallowed it before he ran his tongue over her lips and plunged it into her mouth. Beryl was kissing him back, thrusting her tongue against his before she nibbled at his lip. It was exquisite torture. Her lips were so warm and welcoming. He broke the kiss and nibbled her lower lip.

Theodore whispered in Beryl's ear. "You will be the death of me this night. We must stop."

He brushed his lips against her for the final time. "Have a good night, Beryl, and I will see you in the morning."

Beryl smiled, a very mischievous look in her eyes. What was she thinking?

"Goodnight, Theodore." She went to the door and paused but did not look back. She opened the door and faded into the night, leaving him with a hard cock.

"Damn it!" Theodore swore.

Regardless of how much he enjoyed kissing and touching Beryl, this could go no further. He would be breaking his promise not to become intimate with anyone who served in his household. It did not help that he knew Beryl wanted a husband. He, by no means, wanted a wife. Their positions were set, and it would be foolish to entertain the thought of anything else. Yet, he could not help but think how comfortable he was with her at Bowden Park. For reasons he could not explain, it felt right. He was happy she was there, and he had her spiteful cousins to thank for his fortune.

Theodore poured himself another bourbon as he waited for his blood to cool. He would have to try harder to keep his hands to himself. But what was more intriguing than his resolve was why she had been so open and responsive to his kisses. What changed?

CHAPTER 13

Beryl returned to her room, and only then did she realize she had not chosen a book. She dared not return to the library. At any rate, she did not think she could read tonight. She smiled. Her body was alive in a way that she could not have imagined before. And the look in Theodore's eyes was one of tender desire. She changed into her nightdress and crawled beneath the covers.

As she lay on her pillow, she was filled with wonder at how her body responded to Theodore's touch. She did not know it was possible to feel all those delightful shivers when his fingers explored her. Beryl did not know she could feel wet between her thighs and such tension in the pit of her belly.

She was eager for him to explore her, and she felt a fire ignite inside her when he touched her soft flesh.

When they kissed, his tongue sent shivers of desire racing through her, and the pit of her stomach went into a wild swirl. Beryl had returned his kiss with the hunger that she felt, and she felt she could not get enough of the delicious sensation. Perhaps it was for the best that Theodore had the presence of mind to halt their actions before they went any further.

She was even more curious about him after she saw the tender look of pleasure in his eyes when he touched her. She could not pretend she did not feel it anymore. Not when she was longing for him. Beryl loathed lying and would not deceive herself.

She was falling for the viscount, and it was a frightening awareness. *Is it possible that you could fall for me, Theodore?* Beryl silently asked. He seemed to enjoy her company, and he certainly wanted to kiss and touch her. Perhaps when they got to know each other better, he would come to care for her. She liked that he valued her opinion, for he made the effort to spend a bit more time with the girls.

Whenever she walked in the manor, there was a lightness in her step and an eagerness to see the viscount. She yearned for a glimpse of him this past week, and she missed conversing with him and taking some of her meals with him. Beryl suspected that he purposefully avoided her. Her lips trembled. She hugged a pillow tightly against her chest.

He had not given her the slimmest of hope that they could have something more than a liaison. More the pity. If he did not fall in love with her, and she gave herself to him wholeheartedly, she risked being ruined. She would probably not be able to get another favorable position and doubted she would be able to rebuild her reputation. There was a lot at stake.

Theodore was wealthy and handsome, and she had seen the changes in him. He was more attentive to Louise and Mattie and had hardly left the estate, giving his business affairs due attention. At first, she though he was nothing but a rake, yet she discovered he was intelligent, articulate, and witty. She greatly enjoyed his company. She found herself thinking about him when she lay in bed at night. He left a vivid impression on her imagination and was slowly burrowing deeper into her heart and hopes.

Beryl's eyelids grew heavy, and she drifted off to peaceful sleep.

The following morning, Beryl awakened feeling

refreshed. She quickly performed her morning ablutions and got dressed. She went to the tutor room and had breakfast with the children. They quickly ate, and Beryl smiled at how eager they were to be with her.

"Miss Louise and Miss Mattie, today we will use a slate for our lessons."

Both girls giggled. "What is a slate?"

Beryl went to a trunk in the back of the room and retrieved two slates and pieces of chalk. "This is the slate and this is chalk. We are going to start by learning to write the letters of the alphabet, and it is these letters that we will use to spell words."

"Apabet?" Mattie asked, her cherub face scrunching in a frown.

"No, alphabet, silly," Louise replied.

"Repeat after me, Mattie, A-L-P-H-A-B-E-T, Alphabet."

Mattie repeated each letter after Beryl and finally the word. She beamed, and Louise applauded her. Beryl prepared a cloth for each girl to clean the slates. Beryl had a slate of her own, and she used it to write letters and then asked the girls to follow. She sometimes held Mattie's hand to help her form the letters, but Louise was a quick learner. Beryl continued with the lessons until lunch. After lunch, the girls had a nap, and Beryl decided to walk in the garden.

She wondered if she would run into Theodore as she descended the stairs. She did not. She had just opened the door when a carriage pulled up, and an older, distinguished gentleman alighted. Immediately, Beryl could see the resemblance. He had salt and pepper hair, a neatly trimmed beard, and a mustache. He was just as tall as Theodore but leaner, and Beryl knew it was his uncle.

He bowed. "Lord Amos Merton, at your service."

Beryl stifled a smile as she hardly thought he could be of any service.

"Lady Beryl Keene, the governess. I am pleased to meet you, Lord Merton."

"The pleasure is mine. I wish to express my condolences for your loss. Lord Penrose was a distinguished lord. It was such a shame what happened," Lord Merton said.

Beryl smiled. She could see that Lord Merton was a bit of a character. "It is very kind of you to say so, Lord Merton. Louise and Mattie are having an afternoon nap so I will take a turn in the garden."

Lord Merton scrutinized Beryl, and she wondered what he was thinking.

"I see. Let me not delay you further, but I will stay for dinner; please join us."

"Thank you. I will see you then," Beryl said as she walked toward the garden path.

She could feel Lord Merton's eyes burn a hole in her back, but she refused to look in his direction. Beryl started thinking about what she would wear to dinner before she stopped herself. It did not matter. It was not as if she was meeting her future in-laws. So, it mattered not what the uncle thought of her in that sense. His only concern would be if she were a good governess, and she understood he may have some influence with Theodore. She could easily be replaced.

Beryl kept her walk short. She returned to her room for a short spell because she had not finished unpacking and wanted to choose a dress for dinner. Although she said she would not think about it, her nerves were a bit rattled. She was fretting about dinner. She was relieved when the maid came to tell her the children were awake. Beryl returned to the tutor room and continued lessons until it was time for the girls to have their meal.

Beryl returned to her room and washed her

hands and face. She changed into an emerald-green dress with a low neckline and puffed sleeves. She had easily admitted to herself that she was a bit anxious about dinner with Lord Merton, but Beryl was also thinking about Theodore because she had not seen him since they kissed … and more, last night.

She enjoyed the time she spent with the children, teaching them letters and sums, but if anything, it made her consider what was missing from her life. She was frustrated by the yearning emptiness yawning wider inside her heart, and she wanted to fill it. Beryl wanted to discover if Theodore could be the one to do so.

She hurriedly dressed, recognizing the time went by all too quickly. Beryl was satisfied with her reflection when she looked in the mirror. It was time. She descended the stairs to the drawing room and hoped that the evening would not be an unmitigated disaster.

Beryl opened the drawing room door, and her heart raced when she saw Theodore. She was sure her cheeks were stained a bright red, for at the forefront of her thoughts was the wanton way she had behaved and the heat he evoked. Their gazes collided and there was an enigmatic look in his eyes she could not interpret. Did he know that she thought about him when she lay alone in bed last night? Did he know that she had a shiver of anticipation whenever he entered the room and a quiver of desire when his eyes fell upon her. These were feelings that no other man elicited. The intensity of it excited yet frightened her.

Beryl took a deep breath and tried to calm herself while she willed the butterflies in her stomach to go away. Theodore was freshly shaven, accentuating his strong jaw. She quickly looked away because she did not want to hold his gaze for longer than was appropriate.

"There you are, Lady Beryl. I gather you have already met my uncle." It was more of a statement than a question.

"We met this afternoon, Lord Bowden," Beryl said with a smile.

"Would you like to have a glass of wine?" Lord Merton asked.

"Thank you," Beryl replied.

He poured her a glass while she glanced at Theodore. His eyes were dark and fiery, and they seemed to glow and pierce. Beryl swallowed. He towered over his uncle by a full eight inches. He held a glass of what she believed was bourbon with hands that were beautiful, long-fingered, and strong. Why had she not noticed those hands before? Was it because last night his fingers …

"Here you are, Lady Beryl." Lord Merton said as he handed her the wine.

"Thank you," Beryl said and immediately took a sip.

"My nephew has just been telling me how fortuitous it was that you met. He was not looking for a governess the last time I saw him," Lord Merton announced.

Beryl had not been uncomfortable around Lord Merton, for he seemed pleasant enough. However, for some unexplained reason, she now felt a bit nervous.

"It was fortuitous indeed," Beryl said.

"Although it has not been long, I can already see a change in the children. Lady Beryl has been a positive influence, and this is no doubt due to her kindness, patience, creativity, and empathy," Theodore said.

Beryl snapped her gaze to the viscount. She had not been expecting the compliment. Her entire body felt warm. "I am grateful for your kind words, Lord Bowden."

Lord Merton arched a brow. "And this is your first position as a governess, Lady Beryl?"

"It is."

"You are to be commended for doing such a splendid job."

The butler knocked on the drawing room door and announced that dinner was served. Theodore led the way to the dining room, and Beryl and his uncle followed. They took their seats and began their meal.

Lord Merton gazed at Theodore with focus. "I suppose now that you have a governess, you will soon be off to your travels."

"Not at this present time, Uncle," Theodore said.

Lord Merton gave a deep, gratifying sigh. "Splendid! You know how I feel about you being around. The children need you. The estate needs you."

"So you have made clear, Uncle, several times, I might add," Theodore said drily, his expression unreadable.

"That was not the only thing that we discussed. When will you be returning to London? If my memory serves me correctly, you were going to socialize with ladies of the *haut ton*."

Bewilderment filled Beryl. Did Theodore make a commitment to his uncle that he would seek a wife? She needed to understand. She searched his face, and it appeared that he wanted to be anywhere but at this dining table. Theodore downed his drink, and a shadow crossed his face.

"Your memory serves you well, but I decided to prioritize being here when the children were introduced to Lady Beryl and having all the arrangements to make."

"And from what you said of Lady Beryl earlier, you have achieved that."

"There are other things that demand my attention more than a wife," the viscount snapped.

Beryl quickly sipped her wine and wished she'd had dinner with the children instead. She was certain Theodore would prefer it if she was not a party to this conversation.

"The steward and I have been having frequent meetings with the farmers' cooperative to discuss the diversification of our crops," Theodore said, diverting the conversation.

Lord Merton's hands stilled, and his eyes sparkled and gleamed. "You do not know how pleased I am to hear you say that."

Beryl was enjoying her meal but listening

attentively to the conversation until her thoughts wandered off. Apparently, Theodore had discussed marriage with his uncle. Perhaps, if he was considering it, even a tiny bit, he would look closer to home.

Hope sparked brightly inside her chest, and she prayed she was making the right choice in deciding to open up her heart to him.

CHAPTER 14

What Theodore felt for most of his life was resentment towards the restrictions associated with the viscountcy. He had felt it for his brother and was relieved that he was not the one to be groomed, molded, and sculpted to become the perfect heir. The life as lord of the manor, a wife and children belonged to William. It was never truly his life. He never wanted it. He could think of all the efforts his father made to reform his supposedly rakish ways. Theodore leaned into the freedom that was afforded him and led a life of leisure and pleasure. That was the life that suited him, and he was good at it. He would not simply marry because it was expected that once a man had a title, he should put the old ball and chain around his neck. Utter rubbish.

"I know you think I am still the misguided young man that father sent off to manage our smallest estate in Carlisle."

His uncle nodded, smiling at the memory. "I recall your father was quite exasperated. Did he not give you an ultimatum to get your life together by either going into the clergy, or politics, or being cut off?"

Theodore chuckled. "I remember it well. It was not much of a choice. Can you imagine me being in the clergy?"

"With your lifestyle what it was, I must say no."

Theodore paused as he remembered his father's stern expression. "I had no interest in politics. It is far too boring."

His uncle nodded. "It was William who protected you from the worst of it. Your brother truly loved you, and I think that deep down he admired your spirit."

Theodore's glass was halfway to his lips when he paused and rested it on the table. His hand stilled and he could feel Beryl's eyes boring into him.

Theodore held his uncle's gaze. "Whatever do you mean?"

"Your father was at the end of his rope, and he was losing his patience. It was William who suggested he give you the smaller estate to manage."

The corner of Theodore's lips lifted into a wry smile. "I should have known."

His uncle smiled, a fond look entering his gaze. "William was always looking out for you. Perhaps he wished that sometimes he could throw caution to the wind and escape the confines of duty."

Theodore's heart squeezed. "You really do believe that?"

"I do. William also covered for you because you managed the estate but only just."

The way Theodore managed, or more accurately failed to manage the smaller estate would not do now. Truth be told, he felt a bit ashamed that he did not make better use of that opportunity. Of course, he learned a few things but he did not apply himself. He could have learned so much more.

Theodore knew what his uncle thought of him. He was nothing but a wastrel heir who favored pleasure over responsibility, whose life did not have a semblance of purpose and meaning. His uncle had often thought to shame Theodore because of his carefree existence, but Theodore never let it deter him. He did not want an existence filled with the weight of obligation after obligation. There was more to life than this, and he would need to discover that for himself. He was the only one that could do this, not his uncle; and it would be on Theodore's schedule. Sometimes he wondered why he resisted so much. His fate was more or less decided when his brother passed away.

Some would say he was a rich, spoiled lord who had never worked for anything. It had all been placed before him on a silver platter. Those who were being really nasty would say he should have been the one to die in the accident. *Fuck them.* Theodore did not think that he was unsalvageable. After all, he had not run off on another jaunt, and he was venturing out on the estate, managing its business as he fashioned life as the viscount.

"Look at the bright side, Uncle. At least I have shown an interest in crops, diversification, and yields. Rome was not built in a day. It will take time for me to adjust to a more domesticated lifestyle, to all of this."

His uncle's eyes creased with merriment. "I suppose you are right. Perhaps the next time I invite myself over you will tell me you have found a wife.

I doubt it, Uncle. Why would I be in a hurry to find a wife when I have Beryl and the girls? Men were keen to marry when they wanted to start a family. Theodore already had his nieces to care for, and, now that he had a governess that they were all pleased with, there was less of an impetus to marry. He suspected eventually he might wed. He wondered what kind of husband he would be. As soon as he had the errant thought, he dismissed it.

He did not need the complication and burden of a wife right now, nor did he want to imagine how his existence would change with marriage. He was trying to change his life, but he would not lie to himself. He was apprehensive about it, and sometimes he was plagued with doubt. He was swimming against the current of expectations his uncle and society had for him. He had never though so much about being the best person that he could be, but what if his stint as lord of the manor did not work out? What if he failed at running the estate? What if in six months' time he felt such wanderlust that it drove him to Bedlam. He wanted to do better, yet he was a bit skeptical about whether he had it in him. To be like William was such a contrast to everything he had done with his life thus far.

If he cocked it up but remained unattached, he could give in to the pull of travel and roam the continent for a few months. Perhaps France rather than Italy. He had made some friends there, and nobody did debauchery better that they did.

Theodore frowned. He should stop thinking about himself. He was no longer the most important person in his life. That place had been taken by Louise and Mattie, and he should be thinking more about what was best for them. They needed him and they needed stability. He must continue to focus on the things that matter such as building on the legacy that he inherited or, at the very least, ensure he did not lose it through his reckless behavior.

As if controlled by a force outside of himself, his gaze sought out Beryl and stayed on her. How lovely she looked tonight. A warm sensation turned over inside his chest, and he had the most visceral craving to simply sit with her by a fire to laugh and talk. Theodore swallowed tightly. It was only when Beryl came into his life that he realized that he was being egotistical and his singular interest had to go. Her assessment had been honest and direct and, to be fair, quite refreshing.

To his credit he had reflected on his self-centered behavior and how it affected the girls. He certainly did not want to harm them. He acknowledged that being on the continent in their time of grief hurt them, and his focus must be on acknowledging that and do whatever he could to make things right.

It was not easy for him to concede this, but it was a step in the right direction. It was not nearly enough, and he would need to keep pushing himself. He thought of how happy they were when he passed by during their lessons, had a meal or played a game with them. It had cost him nothing more than sacrificing some of his time, and he got great pleasure from seeing their eyes shine.

He was not arrogant enough to believe that he was entitled to their forgiveness. He would first have to forgive himself and make proper amends. They should be able to rely on him, and it could not be on a whim. He needed to be consistent.

His uncle loudly cleared his throat, tugging his gaze from Beryl. When he glanced at his uncle, it was to see him volleying his gaze from Beryl to himself.

Bloody hell. Theodore suspected he had not hidden his hunger for her, given the narrowed-eye look of censure his uncle levelled on him. Theodore nodded once and resumed eating the superb meal his cook had put together. He was relieved when dinner came to an end. He went to his room and stood staring through the window into the garden. Theodore could not sleep because he felt consumed with a sense of restlessness and far too complex wants stabbing inside his chest. The only thing he was certain that resided in the center of this storm … was Lady Beryl.

After dinner, Beryl checked on the girls before she went to bed. She ascended the stairs and entered the drawing room that was attached to the girls' bedroom. The carpet muffled the sounds of her footsteps, so they did not hear her approach. The girls should already be asleep, but she heard whispers. Beryl stood still and listened.

"I miss mother and father so much, Louise."

"I miss them terribly, Mattie."

"I wish they could come back from heaven," Mattie said.

Beryl smiled even as she ached for them. Children were so wonderfully innocent and naïve. It was their purity that makes them so special.

"I know you do, but they cannot," Louise replied. "Do you remember that uncle told us so?"

"Yes. I used to go around the house looking for mother and father, but I do not do that anymore," Mattie said.

Beryl's heart clenched before it began to beat more slowly. They were wise enough to know that if their parents were here, they would protect and love them. She wished that she could go to them, hug them to her and stroke their hair. The pain that the girls experienced at such a tender age was unimaginable. Beryl would do all that she could to make them have a bit of happiness in each day.

"It makes sense to stop because you will not find them. Things are getting better, Mattie. You do not cry out in your sleep as much."

"You are right. I have not had a nightmare this week," she said brightly.

"Uncle has said he will stay home and will not travel to the continent soon. That is good news, is it not?" Mattie asked.

"Indeed. I hope that he does not leave us. Although …"

"Although what, Louise?"

"Although we have Lady Beryl now. She will

remain here with us even if uncle goes away," Louise replied.

"Do you really think that she will stay with us?" Mattie asked.

"I do," Louise replied.

Mattie gave a small yawn. "I am happy Lady Beryl is here. She is very pretty and nice, and she takes good care of us."

A thick lump formed in Beryl's throat. She swallowed hard and bit back tears. The poor things.

"Uncle cares about us, Mattie. I think he misses father too."

"Louise, do you think that mother and father are in heaven because I was naughty? Did I do bad?"

"No, Mattie. It was an accident. Accidents happen sometimes, and it was not because of anything that we did."

When Beryl's father died, she felt shock, numbness, sadness, and confusion. She was of age and could understand the emotions she was feeling. How could these small children make sense of it? Beryl pivoted to leave the room. She would not let them know that she had overheard this private moment. She vowed to support the girls as much as she could. She would do all that she could to lessen their heartache.

Beryl went up the stairs and into her bedchamber. She slowly removed her clothes and put on a cotton nightgown. For a long time, she stared at her door, wondering if she should seek out Theodore. Heat burned her cheeks when she recalled how intensely he stared at her during dinner. What had he been thinking?

Seating herself at the quaint writing desk positioned near the window, she pulled a sheet of paper towards her, dipped her pen in the inkwell, and began to pour her thoughts into a letter.

Dearest Flora,

I find myself missing you more with each passing day. I am in good health and have discovered a comforting sense of peace and contentment here at Bowden Park. There's no cause for worry regarding my treatment. Lord Bowden is exceptionally kind and considers the welfare of all his staff with utmost importance. Your recent letter prompted a period of deep reflection on my part, leading me to a truth I must now acknowledge. I have developed feelings for the viscount, feelings so profound and unfamiliar that they leave me somewhat bewildered. The intensity of these emotions is something I've never experienced before, and I find myself falling for Theodore, harboring a cautious optimism in my heart. Yet, there's a part of me that fears these sentiments may remain unreciprocated.

The children are wonderful, and they are a constant joy. Each day I spend in their company only deepens my yearning for a family of my own. This longing fills me with a touch of sadness, as I confront the possibility that I may never experience the bliss of motherhood and a family of my own.

Do not worry that I am in despair, because I am somewhat content living with the girls and the viscount. I am not at all treated shabbily but with care and respect. I look forward to hearing from you soon and hope that all is well on your end.

With all my love,
Beryl

As she finished the letter, she sighed. Sharing her thoughts with Flora felt like lifting a weight off Beryl's chest, even as it also laid bare her most vulnerable wishes and fears. She sealed the letter before climbing into bed, hoping that she might find clarity and perhaps even the courage to face whatever the future held.

CHAPTER 15

A few days later, Theodore held a letter, and he scanned the contents once more. Moreland had invited him to one of his libertine indulgences. An orgy of fun, it said, and Theodore knew what it would be. An orgy indeed. As he fingered the rich paper, the tranquility of his domesticity crossed his mind. He was at home with Beryl and the girls. He had found a sort of peace in this normal existence because it felt good, comfortable even. He had his misgivings. Perhaps he should not go. Beryl's beautiful smile and tinkling laughter flashed before him before he pushed it aside. Mayhap, this would be another in the line of things he would deliberately do only to regret later. *Bloody hell*. It was not like him to feel this sense of reluctance. He decided to go.

Theodore was sure his friends and acquaintances would be there for they had similar tastes. Over the years they perfected the art of debauchery. There would be gambling and an abundance of women, all shapes and sizes, for coupling. One could sample and swap throughout the evening.

The upper crust of society did not need to go to the opium dens. Moreland provided a discreet room for those who wished to smoke opium for pleasure, but neither of them partook in this vice. Theodore could not abide the taste of opium, and he was not fond of any substance that could dim his wit even for a short time. He took his pleasure elsewhere, and he was looking forward to being drained and his body well pleasured. These were the nights he could be whomever he wished and do whatever he wanted.

Many in polite society consider it depraved, yet many gentlemen would be in attendance tonight and they would enjoy it. Such hypocrisy.

A few hours later, Theodore's carriage pulled up to Moreland's estate and he disembarked. He was quietly ushered into the drawing room, which was more dimly lit than at a ball, but not enough that he could not make out the voluptuous woman that reposed on a sofa on the left of the room. The revelry had perhaps worn her out, and her lush flesh was spilling from the thin gown that barely covered her shapely thighs. He would enjoy running his hands up those thighs.

"Finally, you are here, Bowden." Moreland's voice pulled him away from the woman with the ripe breasts. "I was beginning to think that you would not grace us with your presence."

Theodore chuckled. "Whyever not?"

"Well for one, I haven't seen you since the masquerade ball, and you left London in such haste. I have not heard a bloody word from you since," Moreland said as he pinned Theodore with a curious gaze.

"There were matters that required my urgent attention. I could not pass the responsibility to anyone else," Theodore replied.

Moreland peered at him as if he was a rare specimen. Moreland took a step forward and raised the back of his hand to Theodore's forehead. "Are you well? You do not have a temperature, but—"

Theodore playfully swatted Moreland's hand away. "I am fine. I need a drink."

"Let us go to the next room, shall we?" Moreland spun around and Theodore followed.

He had only taken a few steps when a waif-thin woman with raven black hair approached him. Her dark nipples were a contrast to her alabaster skin. She jutted her pert breasts begging to be touched, but Theodore did not stop to engage with her. She opened her legs slightly as if to present her mound to him even for a fleeting touch. He was decidedly uninterested and continued on. Moreland held the door for him, and they entered a smaller sitting room.

Moreland poured him a whiskey, and he threw it back in one swallow. Moreland immediately poured him another and a brandy for himself.

Theodore heard the soft sound of a slap, a whip on flesh. He shifted his head to the right to see bare buttocks as the whip slightly cracked and the recipient groaned his pleasure. He was never one to become excited too early, but normally, Theodore would have a rush from the decadence and blood would rush to his cock in anticipation of the enhanced pleasure. Yet tonight there was nothing.

Perhaps he was indeed ill or he was losing the fierce passion of his reckless youth. Whatever it was, he needed to shake it if there was any hope of enjoying the evening.

There was a whisper of a laugh and a muffled sound as the door opened behind them. Theodore did not turn to see who had entered the room. Within seconds the voluptuous beauty was sitting on Moreland's lap and her full lips descended on Moreland's with passion. Behind him Theodore heard the rub of satin against satin, the whisper of a chuckle, low and intimate. Before he could turn around, he saw a satin sash before his eyes. He was blindfolded.

"I have a surprise for you, Bowden. Chastity will see to your pleasure tonight. She is a great beauty, and you have not had her before. Go on. Enjoy it."

Moreland gave a grunt, and Theodore could only imagine the cause.

He felt the delicate whisper of a touch on his arm which slowly moved down to take his arm and guide him elsewhere. As he took cautionary steps, he was surrounded by a mixture of whispers and sighs. He heard the moans of a couple tupping, and he knew that they were just upon them. The woman squealed her lustful pleasure.

Theodore heard a door open before them, and he thought to pull back. He did not. They moved through the door as Chastity drew him further into the room, to a quiet that now seemed eerie. She was yet to utter a word, and he felt the pull on his arms. He followed until he was maneuvered in front of the bed. She gave him a gentle push, and he sat down on the bed. Theodore had enough of being blindfolded, the darkness, this strange sensation. As if she could read his mind Chastity removed the blindfold, and Theodore waited for his eyes to adjust to the pale candlelight. They were in the green room which Moreland reserved for private assignations if anyone so wished. Many did not care if they openly tupped in the plain view of others so the room was only occasionally used.

He could finally see her face and large brown eyes peering at him expectantly. Her comely features and pouting lips did not stir him. He was devoid of emotion, no sensation, no excitement. Chastity was wearing a thin nightgown which was laced at the front. She loosened the lace and it fell to the floor. She stood naked before him and immediately Theodore stood up. Chasity reached up to kiss his mouth, but he turned away and she found only his cheek. He held her away from him, and he was sure she understood.

"I do not please you, my lord?" Her pout was even more pronounced.

"It is not—" Theodore began before she cut him off.

"I know when I displease a man." Her voice was quiet.

"My mind is elsewhere," he admitted, thinking of another sweet smile and bright eyes. "I should not have come here."

Chastity's face burned the bright red of embarrassment, and she lowered her head. Her eyes dropped to the floor, and her lips were pressed tight. She retrieved her nightdress and draped it over her shoulders. Her voice had dropped even further. "You are certain that I cannot change your mind?"

Theodore looked away in an effort to lessen her discomfort which was plain to see. He was unequivocal and knew why he felt this way. "Yes."

"Very well." She finished lacing the nightgown and quietly left the room.

An unnatural stillness fell over Theodore. He walked over to the desk and cursed under his breath. He ran both hands through his hair and closed his eyes. *Beryl.* While a woman naked before him sparked no reaction, the mere memory of Beryl's face caused an excited flutter in his belly. He did not belong here and was a fool to believe that he did. Theodore had never been so discontented with one of these events, and the only thing that he could think of was Beryl. He had finally found someone who made him see that there was more to life than the pursuit of his pleasure.

He sat down at the desk and rummaged through it until he found a pen and paper. He penned a note to Moreland because he knew Moreland was otherwise occupied. Theodore left the note on the desk where he knew Moreland would find it and left through the back door. If someone had asked him a few weeks ago, Theodore would happily have said he was a rake. He owned the title. Tonight, he came to the conclusion that this was no longer the life for him. Nothing inside Moreland house appealed to him. It was only her … Beryl seemed to own his desires, and Theodore was a bit unsure how to feel about it.

I'll be damned.

A few weeks passed and Theodore was surprised by how content he was at Bowden Park. He had not planned to remain in England for too long, but now he delayed any plans for future travel. Beryl had made him reflect more and more on his relationship with Mattie and Louise. Theodore knew he could do better, and he wanted to try. It was something that he was discovering about himself. Once he embraced the lifestyle of a rogue, but he wanted to be a better person. For one, he was angry that William had been ripped from his life so soon, but he had to let go of this anger. Being angry would not bring William back, and it had no effect on his circumstances.

He would honor William's memory by doing right by the children and ensuring the continued success of the viscountcy. They needed him. They needed nurturance, care, concern, warmth, and affection. He could not provide it if he were away more than he was at home. He had been a damned fool; God help him.

His uncle would have been pleased if Theodore had returned to London to find a wife, but while he was prepared to reduce his travel and pay more attention to the estate, he still did not want a wife. He opened the door to his room, strolled over to a wingback chair by the fire and sank into the chair's plush depth. He analyzed what transpired between him and Beryl and the raw emotion that he felt when they kissed.

The last time he lost self-control, which was precisely what he wanted to prevent. It was a fact that he did not wish to marry and that Beryl wanted a husband. Nothing had changed. Yet, he found himself staring at her quite often and yearning to just be in her presence. It was not as easy as thinking that he wanted her and she wanted him. No. His rational mind knew that they should never share such intimacy, but he could not get her out of his head.

Just thinking about exploring her wet folds caused his cock to stir. She had been so wet and ready for him, so hot, so enticing. Theodore scrubbed a hand over his face and smiled ruefully when he remembered she wanted him to kiss her. To break her rules and break down the barrier between them. How much he wanted to, yet if he had, he would have ended up with his cock buried deep inside her.

All her virtues that he exalted to his uncle were

quite true. He was getting to know Beryl, and he liked what he saw, whether he wanted to or not. Beryl connected with the girls in a way that he had not, and seeing this made him want to make the effort. She understood how William's loss affected him, and she was supportive when she mentioned the changes he needed to make. The effect she had on him was the darndest thing. She did not judge or condemn him.

Last night, he was desperate to cool his ardor as he lay tossing and turning in bed. It was torture. This morning, he decided that he would steel himself so that he could be immune to her sensuality, but after sitting with her at dinner, he did not think that would work. It did not go well. Desire coursed through him, and he desperately wanted to kiss and touch her. Perhaps it would be best to stay away from the temptation. Yet, he felt comfort in her presence even if he could not have her.

Theodore sighed his frustration. It was more a pity that he was not thinking about affirming his future plans. If he were, Beryl would be a contender.

Theodore chuckled ruefully. He stood up, undressed, and crawled under the covers. He willed himself not to think of Beryl's heated passion. He tried, but he failed. He dreamed that she had come to him and that they were lost in a torrent of passion.

Hours later he pulled the curtains back. He was usually an early riser, but he slept late because he had such a restless night. He gazed out at the lawn. His heart squeezed when he saw Beryl with Louise holding one hand and Mattie the other. The girls let go of Beryl's hand and made a dash for the garden. Beryl had remained standing until the girls had gained a considerable advantage before she chased after them. Theodore grinned. He wondered what they were doing outside at this hour. He expected them to be in the tutor room.

Theodore washed, dressed, and went to the garden. As he approached, he heard Beryl and the girls before he saw them. Today, it appeared they had opted for an outdoor meal, with a generous assortment of dishes laid out on a table. "Lady Beryl, sometimes I do not remember everything about mother, and I feel terrible about it," Mattie said.

"I know this can sometimes be confusing or upsetting, Mattie, but the most important thing is that your mother is alive in your heart because you love her."

"But Louise remembers so much more than I do."

"That is because I am older, Mattie. I will have more memories," Louise said.

"That is true, Louise. You see, Mattie, if you do not remember them, Louise will share her memories with you. They are special to you both."

"Yes, Mattie. I can tell you about what mother liked and that will help you to remember her."

"She was happy and always smiling."

"Yes, Mattie. She was," Louise said.

"Louise and Mattie, finish eating so that we can get on with your lessons."

Theodore stepped from the shadows.

"Good morning," he said as his gaze lingered on Beryl. Her gaze swept his face, searching.

"Good morning, Lord Bowden," Beryl said smiling.

Her loveliness struck his heart and he swallowed hard.

"Good morning, Uncle. Will you join us for breakfast?"

"As a matter of fact, I will," Theodore said as he took a seat at the table.

Daisy, the maid, busied herself with preparing a plate for Theodore and poured a cup of coffee.

The girls giggled and went back to eating their breakfast.

"Thank you. You may leave us," he said.

Daisy curtsied before she took the path back to the house.

Theodore gazed at Beryl as he began to eat a warm, buttery roll.

"I trust you rested well, my lady." He hoped she understood the clear implication that he had not.

The butter melted in his mouth, and he quite enjoyed it. There were more fresh rolls at the center of the table, and he decided to have another. They both reached for the rolls at the same time. Beryl's long, elegant fingers brushed his ever so lightly, and it sent a spark of heat through him. It was as though he could feel her fingers exploring his body and caressing him.

"I did, thank you for asking. It was such a lovely morning. I thought we could have breakfast in the garden," Beryl said quickly as she pulled her hand away.

Theodore noticed she had not asked him about his night. He started eating, and as he chewed, he glanced at Beryl and the girls, and he was happy. It all felt right. William had always seemed happy, and Theodore could now see how his sister-in-law and the children contributed to his brother's contentment. Theodore had never felt incomplete, but somehow since Beryl had arrived, he had been thinking more about life. There was certainly much more to it than debauchery and aimlessness.

Louise and Mattie had finished their breakfast, and they became restless.

"Girls, you may go back to the house, and I will be with you shortly," Beryl said as she took a sip of her tea.

"Yes, Lady Beryl," they answered in unison.

Theodore was surprised when both girls came over to hug him. He felt a lump in his throat, and it was difficult to swallow. Whenever he was around before, he usually avoided Louise and Mattie. It was not that he was callous and indifferent; he did not know what to say to them. Furthermore, they did not seek him out, yet today, they were comfortable enough to show their affection.

He returned their hugs and gruffly said, "Off you go."

They scampered away, giggling together and it was one of the sweetest sounds Theodore had ever heard. He glanced at his sweet tormentor. "Beryl, would you like to go for a walk before you return to the house?"

Color blushed her cheeks and she smiled. "A walk on such a pleasant morning would be welcomed, Theodore."

He took the path that would lead them through the garden and to the edge of the pond. The water lettuce and chestnuts floated in the pond, and the reflection of the sun shimmered across the surface. The pond was bordered by the woods, and they walked along the path between both.

"William and I used to play here when we were young. We even managed to escape the tutor a few times when we should be in lessons."

Beryl laughed. "I did not expect anything less."

Theodore smiled ruefully. "We enjoyed the simple pursuits. Swimming in the lake, climbing trees and exploring the woods."

"I am sure your tutor had a few things to say about that."

"We only had each other. There was no one else around, so we were very close." He chuckled. "William had the sharp wit and sensibilities of the heir while I was the mischievous rascal."

"What were some of the things that the mischievous rascal did?"

"I remember convincing William that we

needed to spend a night in the woods with no supplies."

Beryl suddenly stopped. "You did not!"

"It seemed like quite the challenge at the time. We were missed by dinner, and being winter, it was already dark. To make matters worse, it started raining."

"You must have been terrified."

"I was but I refused to show it. William was quite brave when he realized we were lost."

"Good heavens. I can imagine the entire household was in a tizzy."

Theodore smiled at the memory. "They were. The first thing that they did was search the entire house. They had to be sure we were not there before they extended the search."

"You must have given your parents such a fright."

"My mother had a fit of the vapors. We thought father would have been apoplectic."

"And was he?"

"He was not. I remember it well. When they found us cold and drenched, father just held on to us. It was quite a long hug. It was as though he would never let us go."

Beryl shook her head from side to side. "Theodore."

"I know. William never told them it was my idea." Theodore smiled. "I felt a bit guilty about getting the staff in trouble."

"William was protecting you," she said softly.

"Indeed, he was. Everyone kept a much closer eye on us after that, and I suppose, in a way, that was my punishment. We could not roam around as freely as I would like, but William did not mind as much as I did."

They stopped walking and gazed at the pond.

"Well, this tells you I was a bit of a rascal from the early days. I always wanted the freedom to do as I pleased. As time went on, William never got to live a carefree existence because he always had to be perfect. He did not prioritize his own happiness. To be fair, he could not because his sense of responsibility overwhelmed him. He had to be the dutiful son."

He had not shared these memories about William with anyone else.

"But you understood the reasons for this."

"Eventually, I did. Over the years, there was no mistaking that living a carefree life made me feel liberated and free. My life was exciting, filled with spontaneity and leisure. I pushed the boundaries to ensure my life was always exciting," Theodore said.

He wondered if his uncle was right after all. Did his life lack a sense of purpose, accomplishment, and fulfillment? For the first time, Theodore was questioning whether his vanity, pride, and ego were dictating his life. His life of debauchery would probably not bring him long-term happiness, no matter how he looked at it.

"Thankfully, the girls are much quieter than you at a similar age," Beryl teased.

The smile that lit her face caused his heart to hammer in his chest. He was continually drawn to her beauty, and it was not just her enchanting physical beauty. It was the beauty of her spirit and kindness. The teasing smile on her face fell away, and she registered the stillness. They were still for a moment, gazes devouring each other, until he stepped forward, closing the space between them. He reached up and cupped her chin, so soft and lush under his fingertips.

Theodore took another step forward, and they were close, but they did not touch. He did not take his eyes off her. The pulse at her throat fluttered wildly, and he heard her breath catch.

Theodore's thumb brushed her lips. "You make me forget the promises that I make."

"Theodore, you make me forget my rules," she whispered.

A fierce hunger gripped him, but it was different from the hunger he felt before. It was not that he did not want to kiss her trembling lips. Oh, he wanted to, but he was also feeling a tenderness toward her that he could not explain. His need to be carefree did not fit with tender feelings for this intriguing woman. It did not fit with anything more than wanting a casual encounter. Then how could he explain the feeling that he had to take her into his arms and just hold her? If he was frank, he felt the need to protect her ever since he asked her to be the governess. He never wanted her to hurt or to see tears streaming down her cheeks.

Theodore pulled her into his arms, and their gazes held. His heart was beating loudly in his chest, and his breathing grew shallow. He was lost in the depth of her gaze. Theodore swallowed. He pulled her tightly against him so that he felt all her curves, and she gasped. The heat of desire was raging within him, and he wanted to crush her lips to him, but he did not. Shockingly, when his lips captured hers, it was tender and sweet. He slowly savored her taste as if she was precious and fragile. Beryl moaned and whimpered before she fell against him, trying to get even closer.

He groaned when he felt her fingers in his hair, gently caressing.

She tasted so damned sweet. And he couldn't escape the feeling that he might want to kiss her forever.

CHAPTER 16

Beryl could feel the hard length of Theodore's body. She had one hand on his chest and the other in his hair. She could feel the fierce beating of his heart as she felt the tension coil in the pit of her stomach. She moaned as he gently sucked at her lip. This kiss was different from the others. It was as though Theodore was holding back, but she did not want him to. She wanted him to match the fire that was threatening to consume her. She knew that he wanted more, and she wanted him to take it.

Beryl moaned her need, and she heard him swallow. He tasted like coffee, and his masculine scent filled her nostrils. She liked the smell and taste of him, and she knew that she wanted more. She did not want him to stop. The gentle strokes of his tongue were far too wicked, and a fire of desire ignited in the pit of her belly.

He deepened the kiss to something intimate, yet raw and carnal. He nibbled at her bottom lip before their tongues glided together, stoking the molten heat. The tension careened through her body and gripped her in the pit of her stomach. She did not want this tender kiss anymore. She wanted the firm, demanding kiss to disorient her completely. Beryl could feel the warmth between her legs, and she so desperately wanted him to touch her there. She wanted him to make her unleash her passion once more. She desperately ached for it.

Theodore planted soft kisses along her cheek and jawline before he sighed heavily.

"We must stop," he said as he held his forehead against hers.

Beryl did not trust her voice to speak. She knew that he was right, so how could she fight him? Her body tingled with awareness of him, and she knew that he felt it too. The kiss was broken, but his heart still hammered in his chest. She felt it.

"Will you have dinner with me tonight, Beryl?"

Yes. She wanted to have dinner with him tonight and many more nights. She longed to be in his presence, feel his discreet glance when he thought she was not looking. Kissing him was so delightful, and she liked that he wanted to kiss her. She liked the way he wanted her.

"I would like that," Beryl whispered.

He gave her lips one final brush before he walked toward the house, and she was grateful to be alone for a spell. She needed time to gather her thoughts that were racing as much as her heart. Beryl sighed, and at that moment, she did not care about the rules. His allure was too powerful, too enticing. She was at his estate for a few weeks and the longing for more with this man only worsened. No logic or practical inner arguments abated this desire. She wanted him to bring her pleasure again, but it would hardly be in the garden after breakfast. She would see him at dinner tonight. Her skin tingled when she thought about the possibility.

Beryl walked back to the house and went to the tutor room to give the children their lessons. She tried to concentrate, but it was difficult. Her thoughts were filled with his soft lips against hers with that sweet kiss. Time dragged on, and it only heightened her excruciating need. As soon as the lessons were completed, Beryl went to her room to prepare for the evening. She called for water to be brought up for her to have a bath. She dressed and went to the drawing room. Theodore was not yet there.

Beryl poured herself a glass of wine, and she had only just taken a sip when he walked through the door. Everything around them seemed to fade as he walked further into the room. She was so aware of him. When he gazed at her, she did not look away.

"I apologize for being late. I was trying to get too much done in a short time. I finally gave up. There is tomorrow."

Beryl smiled. "The girls and I managed to get a lot done."

His gaze bore into her, and it sent a shiver down her spine. "Truly?"

Beryl could feel the heat flush her cheeks. "It could have been better if I was not thinking about you."

Theodore swallowed. "I could say the same. I am sure we are both famished. Shall we?"

He escorted her to the dining room. They did not touch, and Beryl was ever so conscious of the tension-filled air between them. She was starving, but she wondered if she would ever be able to eat a morsel. How could she possibly swallow her food when her mouth was so dry? Beryl took a sip of her wine, and it did not seem to help. She was relieved when Theodore took control of the dinner conversation, and in the end, they had a pleasant meal.

The servants had cleared away their plates, but neither of them seemed to want to move from the table. Theodore had a glass of his signature bourbon and Beryl had the remnants of her wine.

"I presume you play the pianoforte?" It was a rhetorical question.

All the ladies in society learned to play, and they were expected to provide gentlemen with entertainment. Playing an instrument was often the centerpiece of a social evening in one's drawing room.

"I do," Beryl replied.

"As do I," Theodore said.

"I would never have guessed," Beryl said.

"That the rake's fingers play over the keys and make melodious music? Come with me," Theodore commanded.

He led Beryl into a room she had not entered before. It was another drawing room where a large, decorated pianoforte was the central feature. She was pensive, for it brought back memories of her father listening to her play. She was always expected to perform at social gatherings and functions, and she was often complimented on her skills. She was adept at expressing and distinguishing herself.

"Please have a seat." Theodore pointed to a leather armchair, and Beryl had a seat.

"I know that men do not usually play. I remember my tutor said no self-respecting English gentleman would participate in an instrumental performance, but I always found playing the pianoforte soothing, and I suppose my mother indulged me."

Theodore became even more intriguing. The pianoforte was closely associated with feminine wiles and charm. Was he trying to charm her?

Theodore sat at the huge, shining black instrument that looked like the sky on a cool summer night. He gave her a wide smile before he lowered his head, and his fingers danced over the keys, coaxing impossibly soothing and amazing melodies from it. He seemed lost as his fingers flew over the keys like a lonely star that fell from the night sky. Every note of that tune was weaved with such beauty that Beryl closed her eyes, and it was as though she breathed in the music. She let it flow through her.

"Join me," Theodore beckoned Beryl to sit with him.

Beryl knew the notes and she happily agreed. She sat beside Theodore, and the air was charged between them. The silence was ended by the sweet sound of Theodore's elegant fingers, and as he ended his stanza, Beryl started hers. Notes swirled around in her head. The black and white keys flashed before her eyes as her fingers responded to the time and rhythm. Her fingers had mastered the piece. She played the instrument's challenging scales and cords in a way that she did not know her hands could reach. The melody was slow yet mesmerizing. Beryl's heart pounded faster. When Theodore picked up his stanza, the sound grew louder, and she could feel the vibrations tingling on her skin and reverberating through her core. The louder the melody got, the faster her heart raced as if it wished to drown the sound of the music.

The music consumed Theodore as he progressed through the song until, eventually, he became one with the pianoforte. Beryl imagined the music rushing through his veins while his fingers were flying across the keys. She relished the total experience of seeing, hearing, and feeling its captivating rhythm. It was beyond words. He began pressing the keys with greater force, the hammer thrusting against the instrument strings with more energy, bringing an increased volume until it reached a crescendo. Then there was deep silence.

Theodore stood, and without a word, his powerful hands gripped her waist and swept Beryl off her feet. The feel of his power and strength was tantalizing. Beryl's senses were scattered as he climbed the stairs to her room. Her head rested on his shoulder and her arms were around his neck. Neither had uttered a word on their journey. Beryl's heart beat wildly, and she could hear Theodore's short raspy breath.

Thud.

Finally, the door closed behind them, and Theodore slowly lowered her. As she slid along his body to the floor, she could feel his arousal, and she gasped. He crushed her mouth with an intense desperate hunger, and she returned his kiss with a raw desire that she did not know she possessed. She reached a hand to grasp his hair, threaded through it, and pulled him even closer. Her other hand rested against his chest, and when Theodore groaned, it reverberated through his chest, a shock to her senses.

Beryl was on fire, and it raged in her quivering

belly. Theodore began to undress her with urgency, and their tongues intertwined between each piece of garment that was shed. Every touch was a rough promise. The quivering moved from her belly to between her legs where she ached for Theodore's finger to explore her heat. She desperately wanted ... no ... *needed* him to stroke her sensitive flesh.

Theodore lifted her and placed her on the bed. He stood up and tore his clothes from his body. His broad chest and hard cock caused her breath to catch in her throat. Beryl felt moist heat between her thighs. Theodore crawled onto the bed beside her.

"You are so beautiful," he whispered as he wickedly caressed her breast.

"Theodore," she sighed as he lightly caressed, pinched, and rolled her nipples. The soft sound of his name was full of need.

He lowered his mouth to claim a hardened nipple, and Beryl groaned. Her hands found his hair, caressing, yet pulling him forward for more. She arched her body against his hard frame and yearned for his fingers at her center. Beryl made a soft mewl when his lips and tongue found the other nipple.

He drew a deep shuddering breath. "So lovely," his hot breath whispered against her skin.

Beryl was thrilled by the intensity of his reaction and the fire that coursed through her veins. It was unspeakably delightful in a way that she could not explain. Beryl had the uncontrollable need to taste him, and she pulled his head toward her. Theodore gave her what she needed, a ruthless kiss that caused her to moan in his mouth. Their tongues clashed and played with each other.

Theodore's hand lightly fanned out over her belly, and Beryl felt she could not breathe. The candlelight flickered over his features, and his eyes were dark with desire. His hands slowly glided closer to her cleft, and Beryl ached. She desperately needed to feel his fingers, but he denied her the pleasure. He glided his fingers over her skin, touching her everywhere, from her nipples to her lower belly. His fingers aroused her, and Beryl arched even more.

"What do you want?" His eyes had not left hers.

Beryl knew what she wanted, but she was not sure she should trust her voice to say it. Theodore's fingers lightly caressed her lower belly just above where she needed him to be. A frustrated sigh escaped Beryl's lips.

"Tell me," he whispered as the emotions played out on his face. It held the promise of pleasure.

"Touch me, there." Her voice was heavy with sensual heat, and her body taut with anticipation.

His finger lightly brushed the folds of her cleft before they parted her sensitive flesh. She closed her eyes and gave in to the pleasure of his finger, which was finally where she needed it. The only thing that mattered as the sensation swept her. Beryl's breath caught in her throat when his finger delved into her hot, pulsing core as he swooped down to claim a firm nipple. His touch increased with fervor like playing over the keys, and Beryl almost shattered as Theodore suckled her nipple and groaned. Beryl trembled when he buried his fingers inside her and gently stroked into her moist heat. When his thumb found her clitoris while his finger was buried deep inside, it almost destroyed her, but there was more pleasure to come yet.

Beryl gripped Theodore's shoulders, and she could feel her damp palms. He withdrew and inserted two fingers and increased the tempo of his long strokes, and when his thumb found her clitoris, she screamed. Theodore groaned and trailed kisses down to her lower belly. Beryl could feel the tension in her body when he kissed her wet folds. His hot tongue evoked even wilder sensations than his finger. She writhed against his tongue as he kissed and nibbled at the center of her. His tongue wreaked havoc on her senses as he licked and stroked deep inside her.

"You taste so sweet," his breath hot against her clitoris before the cool air kissed her. Theodore breathed in her scent, and then he lowered his head to devour her. The combination of his lips, tongue, and the nibble of teeth caused Beryl to forget herself, and when his fingers delved into her, she lost her senses.

Good heavens!

Beryl could never dream that passion could ignite her in this fashion, yet somehow, she wanted more. Theodore raised himself and settled between her legs. Their gazes locked as his cock parted her opening. He covered her mouth in a hungry kiss as he sank his cock deep inside her. Beryl cried out at the invading thickness that suddenly filled her, and Theodore captured it in his kiss. She could feel the tension in his body as he held still. He kissed her cheeks, eyes, and neck before he found her lips again. He had not moved, and she could feel his hardness stretching her.

"Do you want me to stop?" he whispered against her ear.

His hot breath sent shivers down her spine before he pushed his tongue inside her ear.

"No," Beryl groaned.

He kissed her slowly while he moved inside her deeply. His skin glowed and shimmered with perspiration. Beryl could feel his cock deeper and deeper inside her with each stroke. A sob broke from her as she raked her fingers over his shoulders and down his chest. She was wet, and her warm folds yielded to meet his every thrust. Beryl whispered his name. He traced his hands over the contour of her body and raised her hips to meet him. Her breath came in a jagged gasp now, and then there were no more words, just sounds of passion. Together they gasped and moaned.

Her instinct made her clutch him. With a pleasured scream, she found the relief she needed. He had taken her innocence and given her pleasure in return. Theodore blew a hot breath in her ear, then panted her name. He sounded feral and brutish in his heat as he plunged deep into her. He made a wholly sensual sound, a low rumble of pleasure as he withdrew and claimed his release. Her body felt deliciously sore.

CHAPTER 17

He had really gone and done it now. Theodore was not usually one to lose control, but he was desperate to have her. He was still semi-hard as he lay panting beside her. He gathered her against him, relishing the intimacy and their connection. Beryl melted against him. It brought back memories of playing the pianoforte with her. As his fingers danced over the keys, he could feel her body heat and searing passion. The shared heat and sensation thrilled him, and his cock jumped to life. He had desperately wanted to ravish her, and he could hardly wait to get up the stairs so that he could touch and taste her.

His hands were shaking as he undressed her layer by layer with such urgency that he was surprised he had not ripped any of the garments. Beryl felt so good when he whisked her into his arms and took her to the bed. He had settled her gently on the bed, but it belied the passion that was raging inside him. He did not want to frighten her, but his need consumed him. When her gown slithered to the floor, he was mesmerized by her beauty and her soft skin.

Beryl was eager for his touch, such a sensual woman, and he felt her tremble in his arms. Her hands twisted in his hair when he licked her folds, and the scent of her was intoxicating. There was no hiding the musk of her arousal. Her breathy little moan made his cock ache with the need to be buried deep inside her softness. He did not want to hurt her, and it took so much from him to pause after he thrust past her maidenhead. She was so tight that it was almost painful to work his way inside. She did not want to stop, and she moved her hips and urged him to continue. He tried to move slowly, but it was so damned hard.

God damn it!

How was he ever going to be able to keep his hands off her? It would be impossible. Theodore had withdrawn from her tight heat before he spilled his seed, so he did not think he needed to be concerned that she would be with child. He wanted to think, yet he could not clear his head. Beryl nuzzled his neck, and he heard her even breathing as she slept. It had started raining, and the wind howled outside. He could not drag himself away from her warmth.

Beryl purred and threw a hand across his chest and a leg over his thighs.

Bloody hell!

Between the rain on the windowpane and Beryl's warm body draped across him, would he ever be able to get any sleep tonight? Theodore sighed, but it was more of a groan. He closed his eyes and listened to the rain and the wind. Eventually, sleep claimed him.

Theodore slept for only a few hours. He came awake while it remained dark outside, and it was still raining. He slowly extricated himself from Beryl's warm body, which was pressed so firmly against him. He gathered his clothing, quickly dressed, and went to his room. He was feeling drained, so he collapsed on his bed and promptly went to sleep.

When Theodore awoke for the second time, the rain had ceased. He pulled back the curtain and opened the window to the cool morning air. The sky was dark and cloudy, yet he felt that nothing could ruin his mood. He had breakfast and went to the library to see what matters needed his attention. He reviewed ledgers and correspondence until it was time for lunch. He wondered about Beryl, but he was sure that she was engaged with the children. He would seek her out later.

He could not help but think that he had not even bent his cardinal rule. He had broken it, irretrievably. There was no going back. It was a rigid rule which, in the past, he managed to maintain. He had always been so careful not to cross the line with any of the staff in his household, but Beryl had made him throw caution to the wind. He had never been one to be indecisive or flit from one decision to the next. He never had difficulties ordering his thoughts before this woman invaded them. He could not think of another woman who distracted him this much, *ever*. She made him lose his head.

Theodore stood up from his desk. He must eat.

He opened the library door, went through it, and collided with Beryl. They stood still for a moment. Her bright-colored eyes met his, and he could not look away.

He watched her curiously and finally said,

"Were you coming to see me?" Theodore took a step back, and he gave her body a bold, sweeping gaze.

She blinked, and her thick black lashes swept her cheeks. "No. I am playing hide and go seek with the girls."

"I see. Would you step into the library for a moment?"

Theodore did not wait for a reply. He opened the door, and Beryl followed him inside. She closed the door and faced him. Theodore could not resist. Her lips were plump and red. Theodore's finger traced the delicate softness of her lower lip. He brushed his lips to hers, and she was warm and welcoming. Their kiss was long and leisurely, but he raised his head when he felt his cock stir.

"I have thought about doing that all morning."

"And I have thought about doing this." Beryl pulled him into a sure embrace as her mouth covered his. She gave his lower lip a tender nibble, and he moaned.

Beryl broke the kiss and gazed deeply into his eyes. "Now, I must find the children."

Theodore did not want to let her go. "I want to play."

Her breath hitched, and he had no doubt she

understood his double-entendre. Her bosom heaved, and he wanted so much to touch her breasts.

"Very well," she whispered.

"When it is your turn to hide, if I find you before the children do, I will get a kiss."

"And vice versa," she breathed against his cheeks.

Theodore chuckled and followed her through the door. Her sweet derriere swayed in front of him, and he looked around to ensure they were alone before he gave her a small pat. He was thinking of what she could do to calm his racing heart. It was not going to happen at this moment. He blew out a harsh sigh.

Beryl spun around and her eyes flashed. "You will behave."

So bossy and sassy. Theodore chuckled. As they walked down the passage and approached the next doors, he said, "I will take this one."

Beryl opened the door and disappeared into the room. Theodore spent the next hour playing with Beryl and the girls. He had even forgotten he was hungry. Louise and Mattie were thrilled that he was playing with them. Mattie did not let it go unremarked that he had never played hide and go seek with them before. Her tiny voice pulled at his heartstrings, and he vowed to make time to engage in the activities Beryl planned with the children. He was beginning to believe that he would feel more fulfilled by it.

Just when Beryl was making her way back to the tutor room, he whispered, "Have dinner with me tonight."

They stared at each other, an unsettling awareness between them. She smiled, and that was all the answer he needed before she swayed down the hallway. Theodore sighed. It would be a long afternoon.

DOMESTIC BLISS. That was what Beryl, Theodore, Louise, and Mattie had settled into. There was happiness and harmony in the household. It had been weeks since they had first made love, and they had been together every night. There were even stolen kisses during the daytime. Beryl had let go of any shyness she had, and she embraced a sense of relaxation and a deep sense of calm. There was joy, and there was happiness, yet something was missing, and Beryl knew what it was.

Theodore was complicated and mysterious. She was hoping that after they made love and spent so much time together, he would have started falling in love with her. Yet, it did not appear that he had. Instead, she was the one who had all her emotions in a knot. She could not truly understand it. She had never desired something so much and thus far it had only led to unfulfilled longing. There were a few times that she caught herself staring at him, and the longing she felt frightened her. Was she not the one who said she would protect her heart?

Beryl had just had dinner with the children. She was keen to ensure they did not think they were being neglected at mealtimes, so she did not take all her meals with Theodore. They had finished, and the children were having an afternoon nap. Theodore had sent for her so she went to meet him in the library. She never pegged Theodore for a romantic, but having played the pianoforte alongside him several times changed that impression. It was so … intimate.

Could it be that he had made a decision about them and that is the reason why he invited her to the library?

Beryl arrived at the library and knocked.

"Come in," he beckoned. He was standing by the window and gazing out when she entered.

"You wanted to see me?"

"Yes. Have a seat."

Theodore went to his desk and withdrew a document. "I have something for you."

Beryl's lips lifted in a smile. "What is it?"

He reached across his desk and handed her the document. "Please open it."

Beryl unfolded the paper and read. Her heart was thumping against her ribs, and she could feel the color rise on her cheeks. "This is the deed for a house in my name," she whispered.

"Indeed."

She took a deep breath and looked up at him. "But why?"

Theodore hesitated and then murmured, "I do not want you to be the governess anymore. I want your future to be protected. I want to be the one protecting you."

Beryl retracted as if she had been slapped in the face. "You do not want me to be the governess anymore because you want me to be your mistress. Is that it? I am certain that is what you mean by you protecting me."

He raked his fingers through his hair. "Will you

at least consider it? I will ensure that you are well provided for, I promise you. You will have a full complement of staff—"

Beryl stood up and threw the document down on his desk. "I will never be your mistress."

Shock crossed his face before his expression turned inscrutable.

"Never!" she said once more, spun around and made for the door.

"Beryl, wait …"

Theodore called after her but she did not stop. There would be no platitudes for her. Tears pooled in her eyes, blinding her as she rushed from the library. Beryl went to her room, collapsed on the bed, and succumbed. She could no longer stop the tears as a hot one rolled down her cheek. In the privacy of her bedroom, she gave in to deep sobs that rocked her inside and signaled her pain.

I am so foolish!

Theodore had torn her heart out and stomped on it. She had not protected her heart, and she was in love with him. Yes, love. She fell for the rogue. It would not have been so painful if she did not love him with all her being.

Beryl's heart tightened, and blood rushed to her head. She swallowed hard as more tears welled up in her eyes and spilled over. In the beginning, Beryl fooled herself into believing that she only cared for him, but it was much more than caring. She wanted a future with him. She craved the domesticity they had. It felt so good, so right, and she wanted it to continue. She did not want anything as badly as she wanted this. Beryl's thoughts were jumbled, and it was as if they were screaming in her head. She could not bear the thought that Theodore did not love her, and he only saw her as a woman to quench his lust.

How could Theodore think that she wanted to be his mistress after everything that they shared? They had gotten closer and developed a strong relationship, but it was only a mirage. It was clear now. She was not valuable to him, and he would not choose her as a wife. She could be a governess and a mistress but never his wife.

Beryl's voice broke miserably. "You have been such a fool. You were never going to be anything more than a soiled dove. He is no better than Lord Stanmore."

These last few days she had harbored all the fantasies about the future they would share together.

Beryl's tears flowed freely and then she started

to hiccup. She had to accept that while she formed a strong, intimate bond with Theodore, it was not reciprocated. Confusion and emotional turmoil burned deep in her belly. Even though she knew he did not want her, she could not stop thinking about his kisses and hugs. Theodore was by no means perfect. He had his faults and vulnerabilities, yet she loved his imperfections. The more they had gotten to know each other, the closer she felt to him. All the walks in the garden, the games, dinners, and passionate nights had all given her a glimpse of what she could have, what she needed.

Why had she thought the gentleman who said he had no interest in marriage would change? Beryl had gambled with her heart and virtue, and she had painfully lost.

She had to take responsibility for her folly. She could not blame it on him alone, and she must extricate herself from the situation; otherwise, she would destroy herself. Genuine fear churned in her belly, pushing aside the warmth and affection she felt for him. Unrequited love. This is what it felt like. Now that she knew, she needed to accept her reality. She wanted Theodore, badly, but she would never be satisfied with the life of a mistress. Staying at Bowden Park was no longer an option. She must distance herself from him because she needed the time and space to heal.

The pain was so great that it robbed her of her breath. Beryl sat up in bed and brushed the tears away with the back of her hand. Enough of that. She sat by her desk and penned a letter.

My dearest Flora,

I hope that my letter finds you well. I've missed you most dreadfully. I wish I was writing to you with favorable news, but sadly not. I have found myself in a quandary and need your assistance in this grave matter. I settled into the role of governess quite well. As I mentioned before, Louise and Mattie are quite lovely, which makes writing this letter even more difficult. They are beautiful girls who miss their mother and father very much, and we have formed an attachment.

Alas, I have been rather foolish, falling helplessly in love with the viscount. He does not return my sentiments and wishes to remain an uncompromising bachelor. I became endlessly fascinated with him and came to enjoy the time that we spent together. I should have been more circumspect in my thoughts and actions, being so enclosed alone with the viscount, but I was powerless to stop my desires from invading my thoughts.

I should not have left my heart so open to a

gentleman who did not wish to marry. Oh Flora, I had hoped that when we got to know each other, he would change his mind. Everything was going famously well. The viscount decided not to travel to the continent, and as he stayed closer to home, he took a much more active role in the matters of the estate. Mattie and Louise were starved for his attention, and he found time during his busy day to play games with them. I thought he would have changed his mind about marrying, but he only sought for me to be his mistress. As I am writing to you, my heart is shattered, and I am confused about loving yet wanting to be away from the viscount.

I am sure you can understand my dilemma, as my position here is precarious at best. Please help me by allowing me to have a respite at your country estate so that I can gather my thoughts and composure. As you can imagine, this matter is quite urgent, for I need to leave Bowden Park for at least a week.

I am eagerly looking forward to your reply, Flora.
Your friend,
Beryl

CHAPTER 18

Beryl did not wait for a response from Flora. Even when her cousins treated her badly Beryl had never dared importune on her friend. But now she needed Flora, for it would be too devastating to linger at Bowden Park. Beryl had approached Theodore to secure one week's leave from her duties and he acquiesced. She wondered if mayhap he understood how infuriated she was at his proposal. For whatever reason, he decided not to discuss the matter any further, and she avoided spending more time than was necessary with him. She needed the space. On the few occasions when they had been alone, she could feel his piercing eyes upon her, and she did not understand what it was that he was searching for.

Why could he not see they were made for each other? Now that they had gotten to know each other, she thought they were perfectly matched. She had such hopes. She wanted him to choose her so much, but he did not. Her thoughts were interrupted by the long-awaited response from Flora.

Dearest Beryl,

I was pleased to receive your letter but ever so sad to learn that you are heartbroken. I was filled with dread when I discovered the reason you wished to flee Bowden Park. You are enamored with the viscount, but he will not commit to a marriage. Dear friend, my heart aches for you, and I wish that I could be there to comfort you. I should have counselled you to guard your heart lest it be shattered, because it will take time to mend. It will not be easy for you to become whole when the source of your pain is with you in close confines. My poor darling, know that I will be there with you in spirit.

Of course, you are welcome to stay at Basildon Estate as we remain in town for the remainder of the season. I have written to Martha, our chief housekeeper, and she will have a room prepared for you, and she will see to your comfort. I know how much you appreciate the outdoors and you are fond of lakes. I am sure you have not forgotten the beautiful Morden Lake. You will find it as tranquil and pleasant as it ever was.

I trust you will find some solace while you are at Basildon Estate, and you will decide what is best for you. Surely, you must be contemplating your future as a governess at Bowden Park.

Please write to me as soon as you arrive. It would put my heart at ease.

Love,

Flora

Now that she had heard from Flora, she would leave shortly, but first she must speak with Louise and Mattie. She certainly did not want them to feel that she was abandoning them. They had lost so much already and had grown attached to her which meant leaving for even a short time would upset them. She had been kind, patient and understanding so the children looked to her for guidance and support. She hated that she had to leave, yet she needed the time to take care of herself, to reduce her hurt and anxiety.

Beryl left her room and joined the girls for breakfast. She felt Louise's small brown eyes gazing at her quizzically.

"Are you well, Lady Beryl? You have not had breakfast."

Beryl looked down at her plate; she had succeeded in pushing the food around it, but Louise was right. She had not eaten. Louise's words caused Mattie to look at her with a forlorn expression. It stabbed at Beryl's heart.

"I am well, Louise. It is kind of you to ask." Beryl rested her fork down and took a sip of tea as if to delay the inevitable.

"What is it then?" Louise persisted.

"You are leaving us, are you not, Lady Beryl?" Mattie piped up and her eyes shimmered with tears that were threatening to spill over.

Louise's mouth dropped open, her gaze accusatory.

"I will be going away, but it will only be for one week."

"A week? A week is seven days. You will return after seven days?"

"Absolutely, Mattie. I will."

Mattie took a long, deep, slow breath. Beryl could see that she was trying to be brave.

Beryl smiled reassuringly. "I know this is hard because we have a routine and it will change this week. But we are going to think of some new special routines together when I get back."

"Can we come with you?"

"I am afraid not, Louise. There is something that I must do alone. I can promise you that when I return, we will have breakfast in the garden if weather permits. Also, I will allow you both to decide on the games we play each day for a week."

Mattie's lower lip trembled. "You promise?"

"I promise. I expect you to be well behaved young ladies while I am away. Can you do that for me?"

"I certainly can," Louise quickly answered, looking pointedly at Mattie.

Not to be outdone, Mattie replied, "So can I."

Beryl breathed a sigh of relief. Rivalry had reared its head so things were back to normal. "Now it is time for your lessons."

The rest of the day passed uneventfully. Beryl had already packed the few items that she would take with her, and she had an early night. When she cried into her pillow, there was no one to hear her. She was alone in her anguish. Beryl awoke quite early feeling a bit apprehensive about her day ahead. She got up from bed and peered through the curtains, but it was still quite dark. Even the birds were quiet at this time of the morning. The flowers and grass were covered with morning dew. There was a gentle morning breeze, and Beryl felt the promise of a new beginning.

She had a long journey ahead so she had arranged for the carriage to be early. She had rented a carriage because she could afford to, based on the generous salary that Theodore had paid her. She did not use one from Bowden Park because she wanted to ensure her privacy for the time she would be away. She had to ask Theodore for permission to leave for the week, but as far as she was concerned, he did not need to know where she was going.

She quietly descended the stairs and went into the waiting carriage. The carriage rolled down the cobble driveway, and she moved the curtain to peer through the window. She watched as Bowden Park faded into the distance. Theodore had gone for his morning ride, and Beryl had timed everything perfectly. By the time he returned, she would be long gone, and she had left no note to say where she was going. She had gone to the children's room and kissed them both on the cheek while they slept.

Beryl unfolded the letter she received from Flora and read it once more. She was grateful to have such a dear friend. Thoughts of Theodore invaded her mind, but she pushed them aside. She knew that it was impossible for them.

***

Theodore returned from his morning ride feeling irritable and restless. He thought a ride was what he needed when he called for his horse. He headed for the lake as he thought about Beryl's reaction to his proposal and the fact that she had avoided him ever since. The ride was supposed to help him think clearly, but he could not. When he arrived at the lake, he jumped from his horse and left him to graze. Theodore stood at the water's edge where it was quiet and peaceful. The only thing that intruded on his thoughts was Beryl. This was their place. He had only shared it with her and, somehow, that made it special.

He tried earnestly to get her to be his mistress. He bedded her and offered her a home and servants. She recoiled as if he had struck her. He recalled the anguish in her eyes when she read the deed and understood what he was asking. Theodore was not overly sentimental, but his heart clenched when he saw her pain. Immediately, he wished that he could take the words back, but rather foolishly his pride stood in the way. It was his bloody ego that led him to this point.

Finally, he could understand what his father felt for his mother because he could say with certainty that they loved each other. His father was kind and giving. There was so much about him that had changed since Beryl came into his life, and he knew that although he had grown, there was still more to be done. This was only the beginning. Yet, if she had such an effect on him in such a short time, imagine what she would do as his wife.

Theodore enjoyed being in Beryl's bed, and the nights that they shared were pure bliss. She enjoyed being with him too, and she could not hide her passion that shimmered under the surface. He only had to look at her with intent or give her a slight touch and it would all come to the fore. He wanted all of that to continue, but did he want more? For once he was not thinking with his cock. He was thinking straight and this is with what he was faced. Beryl wanted marriage, but he had always thought it was never for him. He was torn and conflicted. How could he want to keep her close, to satisfy his every desire, but be unwilling to commit to her and give her his heart?

He was afraid. What if he was trying to be

something that he was not? He was never a hypocrite. On one hand, being a rolling stone and living a life of debauchery was the life he understood well; on the other, the role of viscount and heir was something that he was trying to learn. He felt caught in the middle of two worlds. He did not know if he would make a success of the viscountcy, let alone being a husband. What if he committed to Beryl and they lived in harmony for a while only for him to fall back to his old ways? He was happy with what he truly knew and terrified of the unknown. If he failed, he would ruin everything, including his future family life and there would be no going back. Theodore's stomach churned.

He ran his hand through his hair in frustration. He was undecided and he did not think the answer would come to him today. He needed more time to think about it. It was not an easy decision, and he did not want to rush and muck it up. He wished William was here. They could have talked about it although William made it look all too easy.

His ride did not have the desired effect. It had done him no good, well not in the way that he wanted. He was just as confused as when he set out this morning. Theodore walked away from the water's edge and at that moment he had an unsettled feeling. He could not quite put his finger on it, and he dismissed it as the jitters. Perhaps he was just overly tired. He gathered the horse's reins, mounted, and headed back to the house. He had work to do.

After he returned, Theodore had breakfast and returned to the library. He had to review a few agreements with his tenants and discuss the season's crops yield with his steward. He tried to concentrate, but his thoughts remained unsettled. He stood up from his desk and poured a glass of wine, then sat in the armchair by the window comfortably sipping his drink. At that very moment there was a knock on the door. It was a soft knock so he knew it was the children.

"Come in."

Louise and Mattie entered, and Theodore gave them a welcoming smile. They occasionally came to see him in the library and when they did, he made time for them. It was all because of Beryl. He would never have thought to do that before. He was selfish and his first and last thoughts were about himself.

"Good morning, Uncle," they said in unison.

"Good morning, Miss Louise and Miss Mattie."

They did not giggle as they usually did when he referred to them as 'Miss.'

Theodore stepped away from the window, and it was only when he was close to the girls that he saw Mattie's tear-streaked face. His heart began to pound. "What is it?"

"Lady Beryl is not here," Louise said. Her sad eyes bore into him.

Theodore lifted a brow. "You did not have breakfast with her this morning?"

"No, Uncle," Louise replied.

Mattie was twisting her arms, and she finally blurted out. "Lady Beryl said she would be gone for a week, but I did not want her to go."

"Why did she leave, Uncle?" Louise asked.

Theodore remembered that Beryl had mentioned having a week off, but he did not realize that the time had come around so soon, and she did not say where she would be.

"Lady Beryl had some personal matters to attend to. Do not worry, girls. She will be back just like she told you." Theodore wondered if he was trying to convince the girls or himself. "Go to the tutor room and practice your letters. I will ask your nurse to sit with you."

The girls turned and started walking toward the door. It was Mattie who turned around to face him.

"Everybody leaves … mother, father and now Lady Beryl. I do hope she returns though."

Mattie spun around and ran from the room with Louise following closely behind.

"She will return, Mattie. She will," Theodore said to the empty room.

He rushed from the library to Beryl's room and threw the door open. He stood at the door for a moment before he stepped over the threshold. He entered the room and closed the door behind him. Her room was tidy and the bed pristine, as always. He headed for the armoire and when he opened, he found her garments there. He raised his hand and touched his forehead. His relief was palpable. He caught a glimpse of himself in the mirror, and he did not like the person that he saw staring back at him. He was a bit of a coward.

Theodore walked over to the bed and fell face down on the pillow, inhaling the scent of her perfume. Why was he so afraid at the thought of marrying her when he knew that he had developed an emotional attachment to her? When he knew that life without her felt dull and unbearable? Theodore sat bolt upright. He must find her.

Perhaps she left a note for him. He stood up and went to her writing desk. The surface was empty, but when he pulled the drawer open, he found a letter addressed to him. He reached for it with trembling hands and tore it from the envelope. It was in her perfect penmanship, and Theodore poured over its contents again and again.

He had gone back to being Lord Bowden.

Dear Lord Bowden,

Further to our discussion, I shall return in a week's time.

Sincerely,
Lady Beryl

Was that all she had to say? Those few words?
Damn it all to hell!
It was all his fault. When he called after her in the library, he should have insisted she stayed. He should have explained how he felt. He had never felt such a jolt to his system when he left any of his lovers. He had never missed any of them because he had never let any of them get close to him. He had never trusted and respected them nor opened his heart. He did not want to accept that he would never have her here anymore. He already longed

for her smiles and conversation and everything else that existed between them.

They had already been living under the same roof for months. If, God forbid, she never returned, Theodore could imagine being without her for years to come. He had never before in his life felt the level of contentment he felt in this house with Beryl. And now, because he was unable to commit to her, he would lose her forever.

What the hell was he going to do if he was not able to find her?

CHAPTER 19

When Beryl arrived, the warmth of Basildon Estate greeted her, and she needed it, for she was weary from travel. Only the staff was present because everyone else was in town, but Beryl did not mind because she welcomed the solitude. When would she forget the pain and shame she felt standing in the library, holding the deed? It was as though the deed was the symbol of the foolish notion that she could be Theodore's wife. It laid her dream to rest, and she had no one to blame but herself because he did not deceive her. Theodore never said he wanted a wife, and he had not even hinted at changing his mind.

Beryl was shown to a well-appointed bedroom, and shortly after, a bath was prepared for her. The maid had brought her a light supper which she ate in the bedroom before she sat by the window staring into the night. If she lived in a perfect world, men would not have all the power, she would not have been disinherited, she would have rights, and she would not need a husband to protect her. But this was not a perfect world. She had no means, no money, and that meant limited opportunities to improve her circumstances.

Everything had been going so well at Bowden Park. She had fallen in love with Theodore, and she could not stop it. If she was honest with herself, she had not tried. She loved and cared for the girls, and she dared to dream of marriage. Her mind whirled, and there was a hollow ache inside her chest when she understood it was not to be. Theodore had been unequivocal. There was nothing for them beyond an affair. She loved him, and this was a bond that could not be easily broken, for she was attached to him. Yet, she had to find a way to be free. She knew that she must, but that did not stop the brutal ache that she felt inside. The intensity caused her heart to squeeze, and a harsh sob escaped her.

A part of her wanted to tell him how she felt, but she did not dare. She was afraid to say how much he meant to her and lay her heart bare. Yet, she could not deny the feelings she held in her heart. It was clear her feelings were not reciprocated, and she was unsure if they would be met with derision. There was a place inside her that yearned for a family, and that place suffered a crack when she accepted there would be no future for them. Beryl did not realize that she had clenched her hands so firmly together until they started to ache.

Beryl supposed she knew what she needed to do all along, but it was difficult to accept it. It was no longer tenable for her to remain at Bowden Park. She went about her day trying not to think of Theodore, but it was impossible. The day dragged on and she finally decided to write to Flora.

My dearest Flora,

I was glad to receive your letter, and I know that I can always count on you. I am truly relieved to be at Basildon Estate, but my heart remains in turmoil. I am entirely conflicted about what would be best for me. On one hand, I am loath to leave Louise and Mattie because they already feel that they were abandoned by their parents and subsequently by their uncle. Theodore is much more considerate and thoughtful with the children, nevertheless they will be deeply hurt. They have lost so much already.

On the other hand, I do not see a way for me to remain at Bowden Park. It would be maddening and not best for my health. My heart will not heal when there is a constant reminder of my hopes and dreams that have been dashed. It will be far too painful. I had to plan my exit strategy, and it was not easy for me. Therefore, I have decided to complete the remainer of the year as governess, but I will not seek to stay on any longer. I will inform Theodore of my decision upon my return to Bowden Park. This will provide enough time for him to secure a replacement and for the girls to get accustomed and comfortable with the new governess. I hope this will make the transition much easier for them.

I will return at the end of the week and when I do, I will ensure that I maintain the professional barrier I so carelessly broke when I fell for Theodore.

Sincerely,
Beryl

BERYL WAS under his protection when he had rescued her from her vindictive cousins, but now he was the source of her pain. He was the one who hurt her, and he needed to put it right. Theodore had gone to see his uncle. He sought his uncle's advice because he did not want to make a mistake that he would come to regret. They sat in his uncle's library with a flask of brandy between them. He told his uncle what had transpired up to the point when Beryl left.

"A fine pickle I've gotten myself into."

His uncle chuckled. "I saw the way you looked at her, and it was not as a governess. You could not hide it from me, young man. I have been around long enough to recognize there was something more there."

"I suppose you are going to tell me what a fool I have been," Theodore said.

"Well, someone has to and I am afraid you are stuck with me. Lady Beryl appears to be a woman of good character. From everything you have told me she has had a positive influence, not only on you, but also Louise and Mattie."

"That is so."

"You are happy when you are with her. You are just opposed to marriage."

"Yes, but with good reason. You know me better than anyone, and you have only just recently stopped offering me counsel on my responsibilities."

"And that is because I no longer feel it is necessary. You are no longer that man."

"You speak with confidence, Uncle, but I am not so certain."

"What is it that you fear?"

It took a moment for Theodore to push the word past his throat. "Failure. I do not know if I can live up to the expectations of being a good husband. My life has been the furthest away from this."

"You mistake the matter because you are focusing on the wrong thing."

"Which is?"

"It was only after Lady Beryl came into your life and made you look at the man you were that you started to change. Would you not agree?"

"That is a fair assessment."

"Then why do you find it so hard to believe that with her by your side you can continue to strive to be a better man? You are happy now and you can sustain it. The pleasure you get from your debaucherous behavior will lose its appeal. After you have known this life, the one as a rogue will never be the same."

"There is some truth in that. The last party Moreland invited me to resulted in a hasty departure. I wanted to be at home with Beryl and the girls."

His uncle chuckled and gave him an approving nod. "I am going to tell you a story you may find difficult to believe. Your father was my best friend, who married my sister. You see your father as someone who was hard to live up to, but he was not always that way."

"What are you saying?"

"You are more like your father than you realize."

"My father and debauchery in the same sentence. Incredible."

"Yet, it is true. He was wild and roguish until he met your mother. That was when he matured into manhood, became reliable and emotionally responsible. He remained that way until death. The future became important to him."

"Hmm."

"You demonstrate that your future is important when you can set long-term goals and have aspirations. You take responsibility by recognizing your actions, mistakes, and choices whether right or wrong, young man. You must live with the consequences, and you cannot blame others for your choices."

"Don't I know it."

"You came to me for advice, and the fact that you are not acting like the usual know-it-all says something. You need to think about the kind of man you want to be, the values and morals you want to hold dear. What is it that you really want?"

"I have to decide and I cannot be afraid about making this decision."

"That is correct. Once you know what you want for your future, you will not be afraid."

"I love Beryl. Her absence has made this clear to me. I do not want to lose her. I suspect I have not yet morphed into everything that I could be. With her by my side, I can continue to grow and be a better person. I want her back, and I need to know how to convince her that I am worthy." Theodore ran his hand through his hair and blew out a slow audible breath. "I need to sleep on it."

"You do that. I will caution you that once you have decided, whatever you say is what you should mean. Integrity, young man, I cannot underscore the importance of it."

Theodore inhaled and slowly released his breath. "Thank you, Uncle. I have just figured out how I will find her."

"Anytime, young man."

Theodore left his uncle's estate and headed straight for London. He felt himself to be undeserving. He did not know why he was denying himself happiness. He was not the same man whom Beryl met by the lake on the first day. He was never groomed to be the heir apparent, but slowly he grew to accept the role and the responsibility. He was more gutted by William's loss than he cared to admit, yet he managed to find a kind of joy caring for the girls. It was time for him to believe in himself.

***

Theodore was admitted to the drawing room of Lady Flora Ely. He had given his card to the butler who promptly went in search of Lady Flora. He was far too anxious to sit, and he stood pacing the confines of the room. It was a well-appointed room that was tastefully furnished, but he did not care to note the pieces. He was far too preoccupied with the reason for his visit. Everything else seemed inconsequential. Theodore did not bother to get an investigator to find Beryl because he knew just the person who would have the information on her whereabouts. It was fortuitous that he had a good memory, so he recalled when Beryl told him the pirate at the masquerade was her friend Lady Flora.

Finally, the door opened and Lady Flora entered. Theodore spun around and faced her. His heart was pounding in his chest, and he struggled to control his emotions. He needed Lady Flora's help, so it was important for him to win her over.

Lady Flora arched a brow. "To what do I owe the honor of this visit, Lord Bowden."

"I am given to understand that you are a close friend of Lady Beryl Keene."

Flora gave a haughty reply. "I am."

"She is my governess at Bowden Park," Theodore said.

"I am aware of that, Lord Bowden."

Theodore shifted his weight from one foot to the other. "I must speak with her, Lady Flora. It is important. I know that you know where she is."

"I cannot help you, Lord Bowden. I can tell you she is not here."

"She may not be here, but you know where I can find her. Lady Beryl does not have many friends in society, and she is closest to you. You are the only one to whom she would turn."

"Whyever do you think so?"

Theodore held her steady gaze. "The masquerade ball."

Lady Flora gasped. "I did not think she would speak of it."

"We spoke of many things." Theodore sighed heavily.

"I see." Flora replied, her gaze more assessing.

"Believe me when I tell you that she does not wish to see you, my lord. If she did, she would have left you a letter with her whereabouts when she departed. She wanted to be alone," Flora said.

He was consumed with watching her facial expressions. He would make his point, and there was not time for pride. Not now. There was too much at stake. "I am heartily sorry for being such a fool, and she needs to know. It must come from me, and I do not wish to wait for a week."

Flora's features softened at his words, but he had not succeeded in changing her mind. "I am sorry that I am not able to assist, Lord Bowden."

Theodore could feel his temper rising. "I may appear outwardly calm, Lady Flora, but I am angry."

"*You* are angry?" she said as her brows furrowed.

Theodore struggled to control himself. "Yes."

Flora arched a brow. "My good Lord Bowden,

you were the one that was so arrogant and inconsiderate. You hurt her terribly."

Theodore nodded. "I know it. Apparently, you have heard from her so you know the details."

"I am fully aware of what transpired," Flora announced.

"I am sure Lady Beryl did not only speak about my faults for I have virtues." Theodore scrubbed his hands over his face. I am not afraid to beseech you. I know that I have been a fool, and there is so much that I want to say to Lady Beryl. These are my deepest feelings, and I must pour my heart out to her." Theodore's words were heartfelt.

Lady Flora opened her mouth, and then she hesitated before she spoke. "I have never seen my dear friend so hurt."

Theodore ran his hand through his hair in frustration. "But do you not see that if we are not able to resolve this issue she will be hurt for a long time, and I will be hurt for even longer?"

"Do you mean you will hurt because she is not your mistress?" Lady Flora's hand flew to her lips, and Theodore theorized she had said too much.

The blood drained from Theodore's head, and he flopped down onto a sofa to prevent himself from falling to the floor.

Lady Flora rushed forward, arm outstretched. "Are you well, my lord?"

"Please give me a moment," Theodore inhaled a pained breath. He had not been resting well, had not eaten, and he rode with haste to get to Lady Flora as soon as possible.

Lady Flora blushed. "I forgot my manners. Would you like something to drink?"

"A bourbon, thank you."

Lady Flora poured and handed him the drink.

"I can see that you are genuinely distressed."

"I am distressed. I love Lady Beryl. I want to apologize to her and ask her to marry me if she will have me. So, you see, I need to know where she is so that I can ask."

There was silence. "Lady Flora?" Theodore sighed.

She did not appear convinced. "Lady Beryl has gone through so much."

Theodore took a sip of bourbon. "She has and I am ashamed to say that I know of her pain."

"Well, do you not think she deserves better than the hand that was dealt her?"

"Absolutely." Theodore could not argue with that. "You may not know, but I am a different man from the one I was when I first met Lady Beryl. Please," he pleaded with Lady Flora.

"Very well. Lady Beryl has gone to my country estate Basildon."

Theodore immediately stood and held Flora's gaze. "She has a friend in you, indeed. Thank you. I must make my way to her straight away."

CHAPTER 20

Theodore left London and he had to spend a night on the road. He had a late dinner and retired to his room. He settled himself comfortably into the Grand Windsor Inn, and there were a few things he knew for a fact. He needed time to think about what he was going to say to Beryl. Fact. He would remain in Basildon until Beryl agreed to marry him. Fact. Theodore would not go home to Bowden Park without Beryl. Fact.

He knew where she was, and he should have been able to immediately seek her out, but he did not. Theodore realized he only had one chance to put things right, and he did not want to cock it up. He had to think carefully about how he would approach her for that matter. He thought of going directly to Basildon Estate, but he dismissed it. Theodore's eyes grew heavy, and he decided to think about it more in the morning when he was not so tired.

Theodore languished between being asleep and awake. He sent a letter to Basildon Estate, but Beryl did not wish to see him. She outright refused. She had insulted him by returning his letter, but he would not throw in the towel. He barged his way into the house and he saw her. For a moment, they both stood frozen in time. He was gripped by excitement and fear. Beryl spun around and broke into a run. Theodore gave chase yet try as he might he could not catch up with her. Somehow, he knew that if he did not hold on to her this time, he would lose her for good. Theodore started running faster and faster. He could hear his heart pounding as loudly as his boots pounded on the wood floor. At one point he thought he was catching up with her. Breathless, he exerted all his energy on the final push. There was hot burning in his lungs, and he ran as hard as he possibly could. Close, so close. He reached out his hand, but at the last minute he stumbled, and just then she moved further away and disappeared.

Theodore came awake with a start. His heart was beating rapidly as if he had indeed been running to catch up with her. He felt fear and he put it down to his overactive imagination. Yet, he wondered. Theodore was keen to decipher his dream. He believed dreams were actually an illusion of real life and sometimes it was a sort of spiritual connection. Perhaps it represented his feelings of vulnerability, and the fact that he was judging himself harshly. He did not want to feel powerless. He knew exactly what he would do.

The following morning, Theodore awoke at dawn and went to the stable. He retrieved his horse, and it was prepared for him to go riding. This was not just a routine morning. He rode through the woodlands with purpose, perhaps at a speed some would call reckless. His eyes were gritty from lack of sleep. He did not care. He just wanted to get there. As he approached, he dismounted his horse, and led him by the reins. He walked through the trees and tethered his horse where it could graze.

Theodore's heart was beating wildly in his chest when he saw her. The tension in the pit of his stomach flowed through the rest of his body. He closed his eyes with relief and when he opened them, she was still there. Beryl stood at the water's edge throwing pebbles in the lake. She had never looked more beautiful to Theodore. He had finally come to his senses and chosen her, and he wanted her to give him a chance to show how much he loved and cared for her. He did not want her to regret the day she ever set eyes on him.

Theodore urged his horse forward at the same moment Beryl turned around, and he saw the color drain from her face. His heart gave a thump as it was as though he came alive for the first time since that fateful day in his library. He was enshrouded in gray and gloom and it had all lifted. He missed her in a way that it was difficult to express, yet the intense joy at seeing her frightened him. A small smile lifted his mouth.

"Beryl–"

"Why are you here? Have you not done enough? Could I not have a week in peace?"

"I had to see you, Beryl. Please hear me out. For the first time in my life, I know what it was like to love a woman. When you left and I could not hear your tinkling laughter and chatter, feel your kindness and compassion, I was lost. Nothing was the same. I was not brave enough when we first met to admit that I was a broken man. I–"

"Theodore–"

He rushed forward. "Please, let me finish." He drew in a deep breath, and his hands trembled with all his pent-up emotions. "You were the one who made me realize that I had not dealt with my brother's grief. I could only see the restrictions placed on William to groom him to become an heir, and I knew that I did not want that life. While it was understandable when he was alive, it was inexcusable when he died because I should have considered the estate and my nieces. Because of you, I came to realize there was more to life than my pursuits, and I became a better man. You saw it. I did not seek to travel, took a more active role in the estate, and I made time to spend with my nieces."

"Yes. You have changed, Theodore, and I am pleased to see that you have grown. Your nieces need you." Beryl said she was pleased, but she did not sound particularly interested.

Theodore ran his hand through his hair. "My journey was not complete, Beryl. Even in my evolution there is a part of me that felt I needed to hold on to my past life. In that life, I was free of responsibility and commitment. I never saw myself as a husband."

Hands on her hips, Beryl gave him a withering

glance. "You did not see yourself as a husband so you thought I could only be your mistress? Is that it?"

Theodore shifted his weight from one foot to the other, but he dared not step closer. "I have played that day in the library over and over in my head. I can safely tell you with certainty that my mind was roiling with my reaction, and I needed time and space to decipher my conflicted feelings. I was revulsed and ashamed of my actions."

Beryl's gaze bored into him and he felt exposed. "Yet, you did not seek me out. Why?"

"Truth be told, I lacked the emotional maturity to see what was in front of me the whole time. It was not easy for me. I had my inner struggles and challenges, but I have grown and developed. I can show you … if you let me."

Beryl caught her lower lip between her teeth as though she was contemplating. Theodore waited anxiously, yet she said nothing. The silence was deafening. He had to go further and pour his heart out. He would not leave anything behind.

"Beryl, I am pleading with you … please forgive me … for all the pain and hurt that I caused you. I would be the first to say that it was my pride and arrogance that caused me to act the way that I did. I do not seek to make excuses for myself. I want you to know that I am standing before you an imperfect man, but I am willing to grow. I know that I can do it if you are by my side. I can grow with you because I love you. You make me a better … me."

Beryl's hand flew to her lips, mouth agape. "*Love*? You *love* me?"

"Yes. I was beside myself when you left Bowden Park. I already realized how much you meant to me and how much I wanted … *needed* you in my life. I was a fool to think a carefree life could be fulfilling. It was not and, for reasons I cannot fathom, I still wanted to cling to it. My life was empty before you came along, and you made me realize it could be so much more. I was happy when you were there with me and the girls and that is where you belong."

Theodore stared at Beryl whose mouth had dropped open when he mentioned love. Was she surprised or did she doubt him? The former is understandable; the latter he would not allow.

Theodore took another step closer. "You will not know how much I berated myself for adding to your hurt and sorrow. I tore at my chest when I recalled the hurt in your eyes. I should never have been the source of your pain. Rather than harm you, I want to cherish and protect you. You are precious to me, and I will not lose you. I know you do not love me—"

"But I do!" Beryl's words sent a shiver down his spine.

Theodore knees almost buckled under the weight of his relief and happiness. "You do what?"

"Love you. I love you, Theodore. That is why it was so painful for me to remain at Bowden Park. How could I when I had fallen helplessly in love with you? It would have been too painful to be so close to you after everything that we shared. It would have destroyed me if I could not step away for a while. I love you too much."

Theodore fell to one knee.

Beryl's hand flew to her cheek and her lips formed a perfect 'O'. "Goodness! What are you doing?"

Theodore grinned. "I am being chivalrous and proposing to you with the respect that you deserve, my love."

Beryl gasped and the sweet sound washed over him. Both of Beryl's hands flew to her lips.

Theodore reached inside his jacket pocket and

removed the ring. It was a family heirloom and the last one to wear it was his mother. It had a large diamond with a small cluster of gemstones surrounding it. Theodore removed it and reached for Beryl's hand. "I am your knight, humbled before you, and I pledge my devotion. My heart belongs to you and only you. If you give me your heart, I will never cause you such pain. I will honor and cherish you. Will you marry me?"

Beryl gave a resounding, "Yes." Her hand was shaking a little as Theodore slipped the ring onto her finger.

Theodore stood and pulled Beryl into his arms. He understood the sentiment now, about never wanting to let someone go. Now that he was desperately in love with her, her acceptance made him giddy with happiness. He did not know everything about her, but there would be time to learn. They would get to know each other even more during their life together. This would be their new start, and he would never have to give her up.

BERYL AND THEODORE were in a carriage returning to Bowden Park. They had stopped for lunch at an inn but did not dally there. They returned to the carriage and, almost as soon as the carriage rolled away, Theodore went to sleep. He was clearly exhausted, and Beryl realized he had not been resting well. She studied his sweet bodily repose and handsome features and wondered if he was thinking of her in his dreams. She closed her own eyes and did not know how long she had been asleep when she was jolted awake by the bumps on the rough surface. A quick glance at Theodore showed he was not disturbed.

Beryl was moved by Theodore's love and the kindness he showed on their return journey. He could not have been more attentive. She reflected on how much he had grown and the depth of his character. It had taken him a little while to express his true feelings, but who was she to judge? She never told him how she felt, never said she was in love with him and she had been for a while. If her long-term plan had materialized, she would have left Bowden Park and lost Theodore. It would have destroyed her. Instead, he declared his love and loyalty. He chose her to be his wife. Beryl had never been in love, and she did not know it was possible to love someone so much, not until she met Theodore. Emotion tore through Beryl's heart and tears stung her eyes. She could not bear the thought of anything tearing them apart, and she was certain she did not want to lose him.

Beryl reached out and lightly brushed his cheeks. "My darling. I love you more than you can ever know." It was all she could manage as her voice trembled. Beryl pulled the curtain aside and peered through the window at comfortable familiarity. The corners of her mouth lifted in a warm smile as the carriage entered the grounds of Bowden Park, and Beryl felt like she was home. She had only been gone for a few days, but she missed the children and the estate. As the carriage approached the courtyard, Beryl could see that Louise and Mattie were waiting outside. They were holding something, but she could not discern what it was. As she grew closer, she saw the girls holding a welcome sign and, when the carriage pulled into the courtyard, she could see what it said.

Emotion squeezed Beryl's heart, and tears of joy found their way to her eyes. Theodore came awake when the carriage stopped and they alighted.

The sign read *'Will you marry us?'*

For a moment Beryl was at a loss for words until Mattie said, "Will you marry us, Lady Beryl?"

Beryl fell to her knees and hugged both girls. "I will marry you, my sweet."

"And you will be our aunt. I am so happy, Lady Beryl," Louise said.

"As am I," Theodore said.

EPILOGUE

Nine months later
Bowden town house, London

It was the first ball of the season and the first time that Beryl would be presented as Viscountess Bowden. Earlier when she donned her yellow silk gown, she thought how truly beautiful and radiant she looked. The dress clung to her delicate curves and the color complemented her pale skin, accentuating her beauty. Theodore had looked at her with longing when he came to escort her to the carriage.

"You are stunningly beautiful, wife." Theodore lowered his head and captured her lips in a kiss that left her breathless.

"Behave," Beryl said as she broke the kiss.

Theodore groaned. "We must go, otherwise we may not make it at all."

Beryl giggled and placed her hand in the crook of his arm as they departed.

Now that they stood in the entrance of the Whittington's drawing room, there was a flutter in her stomach, but she had no time to give in to her nerves. They were announced, and she gripped Theodore's hand as they descended into the drawing room. There was excited chatter as the crowd parted to make way for them.

Beryl's eyes scanned the crowd until she found her cousins. Lady Ellsworth and Grace were both here but Estelle was not. Apparently, Grace had not found a suitor last season so she was hoping for better luck this time around. They must have been terribly disappointed, and Estelle would be miffed not to have her own launch this season. Lady Ellsworth thought it prudent to have Grace wed first before turning her attention to Estelle. Perhaps if they were kinder people, the outcome would have been different.

Theodore and Beryl were moving through the crowd, and she could feel Lady Ellsworth and Grace's gazes boring into her. At one point she glanced in their direction and, when she met their gazes, they were venomous. They were acting like the poisonous snakes they were. Ignoring them, Beryl steered Theodore in the opposite direction as they greeted and conversed with the other attendees.

Beryl overheard one of the ladies they had not met whisper. "Do they not make a handsome couple."

"Indeed," her companion said.

Theodore led Beryl to the dance room, and it was the opportune time. The orchestra started the Viennese waltz, and many couples took their place on the dance floor.

"May I have this dance?" Theodore was devilishly handsome, and he had a wicked smile.

Beryl's heart fluttered. "You can have as many dances as you like."

He held out his hand, and Beryl placed hers in his as he walked her onto the dance floor. The orchestra started up, and when Theodore took her into his arms she felt cared for and protected. As they twirled and swirled across the floor, Beryl felt the eyes of the *haut ton* focused on them. As they danced, she caught sight of none other than the Marquess of Penrose, her distant cousin who had inherited her father's estate and unceremoniously threw her out of her childhood home. He was standing at the edge of the dance floor, and Beryl was certain that he was wondering how she had such a change of fortune.

Beryl smiled and gazed into Theodore's eyes. She had what she valued most … the girls and a husband who loved and cherished her.

Thank you for reading ***The Viscount's Daring Cinderella***!

Dark-an Press hopes you enjoyed the journey to happy ever after for the hero and heroine. Our goal is to 'Empower diverse voices, one story at a time.' If you would like to connect with us to keep up to date as we release more stories, have giveaways, and so much more, you can do so via Facebook, TikTok and Instagram.

Reviews are also gold to authors, and we would appreciate your honest feedback on Amazon, Goodreads, and even Bookbub.

Thank you!

The Darkan Press Team

THE VISCOUNT'S DARING CINDERELLA

Read the Series today

The next book in the Damsel in Distress series is ***Her Beastly Duke***.

Click Image to Order!

If you enjoy sensual and heart-warming romance, download a copy of ***A Pocket Full of Mischief*** by Alyssa Clarke!

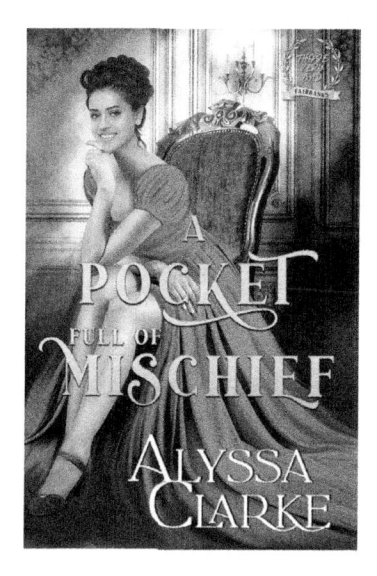

Click Image to Order!

A Sensual Opposites Attract

Miss Penny Fairbanks had always stood out with her vibrant spirit and penchant for mischief. However, to support her infamous family's attempts to find their place among the ton, she reluctantly agrees to adopt a more subdued demeanor, practicing decorum and modesty. Until a haughty viscount callously insults her sisters, igniting Penny's ire and determination to see him humbled.

Her new goal: bringing down the arrogant viscount!

Little does she know, her path is about to cross

with the Duke of Shrewsbury, a man whose stunning good looks and irresistible charm are matched only by his reputation. When he unexpectedly decides to intervene in her quest for vengeance, Penny becomes locked in a captivating battle of wits with the duke, filled with thrilling, sensual encounters.

Soon, Penny finds herself falling in love with a gentleman whose distinguished family may never accept her as worthy of becoming the Duchess of Shrewsbury.

ABOUT HAYLEIGH

Hayleigh Mills became passionate about romance when she started reading Mills & Boon in her late teens. She is an avid reader of historical romance including the medieval period. Hayleigh pursued a career in the medical field but maintained a strong affinity for all things historical. She made the bold decision to relinquished practising to follow her dream of becoming an author of historical romance.

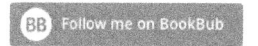

Follow me on BookBub